"Oh, what a cutie pie. He has his mommy's chin," the woman exclaimed.

"And his daddy's nose," the other woman said. "You must be very proud."

Tyler blinked in confusion. They obviously thought he and Eva were the baby's parents.

Eva inhaled a sharp breath. Even in the darkness, Tyler could see her face flush beet red with mortification.

"Oh, but we're not… I mean, we aren't…" Eva stammered.

"What's his name?" the first woman asked.

"Cody," Tyler supplied.

"What a perfect name for a perfect baby."

The women smiled with admiration. When they moved on down the sidewalk, he finally exhaled. They were completely oblivious that their words had caused anyone any discomfort.

He turned to Eva. For a flashing moment, he saw intense misery in her eyes.

"Eva, are you okay?" he asked.

"Yes, I was just thinking about…" She hesitated and gave a sad little laugh. "Oh, it's nothing, really. Just ignore me."

But he knew. All the things she wasn't saying, and he still knew it had something to do with her broken engagement and being left at the altar with no groom.

* * *

Lone Star Cowboy League:
Bighearted ranchers in small-town Texas

Leigh Bale is a *Publishers Weekly* bestselling author. She is the winner of the prestigious Golden Heart Award and is a finalist for the Gayle Wilson Award of Excellence and the Booksellers' Best Award. The daughter of a retired US forest ranger, she holds a BA in history. Married in 1981 to the love of her life, Leigh and her professor husband have two children and two grandkids. You can reach her at leighbale.com.

A Doctor
for the Nanny

Leigh Bale

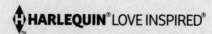

Special thanks and acknowledgment to Leigh Bale for her contribution to the Lone Star Cowboy League miniseries.

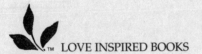 LOVE INSPIRED BOOKS

Recycling programs for this product may not exist in your area.

ISBN-13: 978-0-373-87991-5

A Doctor for the Nanny

Copyright © 2015 by Harlequin Books S.A.

www.Harlequin.com

Printed in U.S.A.

And therefore will the Lord wait, that He
may be gracious unto you, and therefore will
He be exalted, that He may have mercy upon you:
for the Lord is a God of judgment:
blessed are all they that wait for Him.
—*Isaiah* 30:18

Many thanks to Gary and Judy MacKay for their ranching expertise. You two are amazing!

Chapter One

Eva Brooks opened the oven door and peered inside. A blast of heat struck her in the face and she pulled back quick. The biscuits looked as flat as pancakes, yet they'd been in there for thirty minutes already. Maybe they needed more time. Maybe the oven wasn't hot enough. But weren't Martha Rose's biscuits usually golden brown by now? These biscuits still looked anemic white, like pieces of chalk.

Eva closed the oven door, feeling dismayed. "They're not done yet."

Martha Rose, the head cook at Stillwater Ranch, showed a doubtful frown. "Let me see them."

Eva stepped aside. Martha Rose jerked open the door, released an impatient huff, then snatched up an oven mitt and pulled out the pan of biscuits. She set them on the counter with a clatter.

"Darlin', you can bake these biscuits until the Second Coming, and they're never gonna get any fluffier than that. You obviously forgot to put in the baking powder."

Eva's face heated up like a flamethrower. She clenched her eyes closed. A feeling of mortification rushed over her. There was no doubt about it. She was no cook. Never had been, never would be. And it was time she faced up to it.

"Oh, no, Eva! You're supposed to be caramelizing those onions, not incinerating them."

Eva whirled around and gaped in horror at the stove top. Martha Rose pointed a plump finger to where the gas flame flickered beneath the bottom of a blackened skillet. The pungent odor of burning onions filled the air. Eva's nose twitched. She shook her head and groaned. The beautiful onions she'd carefully chopped up had shriveled into little black spikes that popped around in the hot pan.

She clasped the handle of the skillet to remove it from the heat…and promptly let go. "Ow!"

She shook her hand. Tears of pain and embarrassment burned her eyes. Before she could decide what to do, she found her wrist clasped in a strong grip and was propelled toward the sink. A masculine hand reached out and cranked on the faucet all the way. A gush of cold water rinsed her burned fingers. She felt immediate relief and looked up. Tyler Grainger stood close beside her, holding her hand beneath the spray of water. His hazel-green eyes locked with hers. She stared, dumbfounded, and wondered vaguely what he was doing here. Tyler was a doctor. A pediatrician. He must have been making a house call. But she didn't move. Not with his tall frame pressed against her side. As she gazed into his eyes, a giddy sensation swirled around in her head. She felt locked there. Suspended in time.

"Feel better?" His deep voice filled her ears.

All she could do was nod.

He flashed a crooked smile. A smile she recognized as well as her own. After all, she'd known this man her entire life. And with no siblings of her own, she'd idolized him. Oh, yes. With good reason. He'd been one of the star athletes in high school, the valedictorian, school president and winner of every science fair. Not to mention his tanned good looks. She'd always admired him. Depended on him, even. Having him witness her failure in the kitchen made her humiliation all the more complete.

"Put some ice on the burns and I'm sure you'll be fine." His voice sounded low, like rumbling thunder.

Though she was still bent over the sink, Eva's gaze swept him. A thatch of blond hair fell over his high forehead. His eyes sparkled as he released her wrist and stepped back to dry his hands on a clean dish towel. His gray Western shirt stretched taut across his muscular arms and torso. He wore faded blue jeans that hugged his long legs like a second skin. With his scuffed cowboy boots he was dressed like an ordinary ranch hand. Except he wasn't, not with a medical degree.

But even though he was one of the most eligible bachelors in Little Horn, Texas, he apparently wasn't interested in the young ladies of the community. He'd returned to the area almost a year earlier, running a small medical office out at his family ranch nearby. But he never dated. Never escorted any woman down

Main Street. In a town this size everyone knew everyone else's business. And rumor had it that Tyler would be leaving for Austin right after the Thanksgiving holiday.

In four short weeks.

"What are you doing here?" she blurted.

"Paying a house call. Miss Mamie's worried about the baby. I heard the commotion here in the kitchen and thought I might be able to help," he said.

The baby. Three-month-old Cody, who had been left on their doorstep recently with nothing more than a cryptic note that read "Your baby, your turn."

Obviously one of Eva's two cousins had dallied where they shouldn't have and Cody had been the result. But with Ben and Grady both out of reach for now, no one had any idea who the mother was. Thankfully the soft blanket left with the baby had his name embroidered on it, or they wouldn't even have known what to call the poor little tyke.

"Thanks for your help," Eva murmured.

"My pleasure." Heading for the door to the living room, Tyler reached out and snatched a grape out of a bowl sitting on the counter. He popped the fruit into his mouth and grinned. With a pleasant nod, he exited the room.

Watching him go, Eva felt a melting warmth flood her veins. Tingles of excitement coursed up her arm from where he'd held her hand. She shook her head, trying to focus on the present. What on earth was the matter with her? At the age of twenty-five she wasn't a young girl anymore, and she certainly didn't find the man that attractive.

Okay, maybe she did. But that didn't make a difference. He was a friend, nothing more. Besides, after her fiancé had dumped her at the altar six months earlier, she'd promised never to trust another man.

"Humph. I'm glad someone in this house has a lick of sense," Martha Rose said as she switched off the stove burner.

The matronly woman thrust open the window by the sink and waved her arms at the cloud of smoke, letting the fresh air clear the stinky room. With an oven mitt, she clasped the skillet and set it out on the back porch to cool. Then she jerked open the freezer, poured some ice into a clean dishcloth and thrust it at Eva.

"Here. Put this on your hand." With several quick twists of her wrist, Martha Rose shut off the water faucet.

Eva dried her fingers, feeling awful. She'd tried so hard to learn how to cook, but it was a catastrophe every time.

"I'm sorry, Martha Rose," she said.

Martha Rose planted her hands on her thick waist and studied Eva for several moments with a critical eye. "Look, darlin', you know I love you. But you're just no good in the kitchen."

Oh, no. Eva knew what was coming next, and a sinking dread settled in her chest. "Maybe I can stick to washing fruits and vegetables. And I can set the table. I'm good at those chores."

The matronly woman inclined her head, conceding that point. "But you can't peel potatoes and carrots. You nearly took off your finger the last time, and you peeled off more than the potato skins. We hardly had enough potato to put in the pot to boil. It was a good thing I'd made extra rolls."

Eva blinked, knowing Martha Rose was right. But she had to do something to help out here at Stillwater Ranch. After all, her cousin Ben had been so generous in offering to let her stay. If only she hadn't given up her apartment in town. She doubted she could get her old job back as a waitress at Maggie's Coffee Shop. Eva had seen the pleased look in Maggie's eyes when she'd given notice just before her wedding date. No doubt Maggie had been glad to see her go. Heaven only knew how many dishes Eva had dropped and bagels she'd burned while she'd worked there. And she'd ruined enough pots of coffee to last a lifetime. But she'd been tops at customer service. Even so, she should be married now and settled into her former fiancé's home, not mooching off her cousin's generosity. If Ben hadn't offered her a job and a place to stay, she'd have nowhere to go. She had to make this work. Had to find something she could do right.

"I don't think this is a good fit, darlin'," Martha Rose said again.

"I'll do better. I promise. I never make the same mistake twice," Eva said.

But that wasn't the problem. Eva always learned her lessons. But her mistakes were doozies. Such as driving the tractor, taking the turn too wide and tying up the side rake in the barbed-wire fence. Another time she'd mistakenly grabbed a bucket of rolled corn instead of oats to feed the horses. Thankfully, one of the ranch hands had caught her before she'd made the horses sick. She'd then found herself sequestered in the kitchen, but that hadn't proved to be much better. But the biggest mistake of all, the one she'd never re-peat again, was falling in love. Never would she trust another man with her deepest, darkest secret. Never would she hope that he would love her for herself and not the children she could never give him.

As if on cue, a baby's cry permeated her muddled brain. Her heart wrenched with the sound. She in-stinctively wanted to run to Cody's nursery and pick him up, but she forced herself to stay put. No sense in torturing herself.

"Please give me one more chance, Martha Rose," Eva pleaded.

The woman placed a gentle hand on her shoulder and met her eyes. "Darlin', you and I both know it isn't gonna work. We might as well not pretend. With all this trouble in the town, cattle rustlings and steal-ing, those burnt onions and flat biscuits are the least of our worries. It's not the end of the world. But it's time for you to go and do something else."

True, but it went deeper than that for Eva. Her heart still stung from being rejected by her fiancé. In this small community, most of the ranchers valued family and children above everything else. Except their land and cattle, which they wanted to pass on to their kids one day. If she couldn't have children, what good was she? No man in the area would ever want her. And she wasn't about to leave town. She loved Little Horn. She'd been born and raised here. The thought of leaving to try to find a husband left her feeling cold and empty inside. She had to develop a career and learn to make it on her own. There must be something she was good at.

"Why don't you go and help Miss Mamie with the baby? She's got her hands full with that little one, and she could sure use the help," Martha Rose said.

Eva shook her head. "No, anything but that. Not the baby. Please, Martha Rose."

A spear of panic pierced Eva's chest. Lots of people in town knew that she'd been gored by a bull when she was only sixteen years old. But they didn't know that the horrifying incident had left her barren. Unable to have children. And no one knew how badly it hurt her to be around kids…the one thing in life she wanted most and could never have. Not without adoption or taking in foster kids. She had loved and admired her father and couldn't imagine raising her own child without a daddy. She'd have to be married first, which brought her back to the problem of finding a man in this small community who was willing to marry a woman who couldn't give him biological children. And she couldn't take in foster kids when she didn't even have a home of her own.

"Land's sake, it's just a small baby. And babies are easy to love," Martha Rose insisted.

That was just the problem. Eva didn't want to love Cody. Or any child, for that matter. But Martha Rose seemed oblivious to Eva's anguish. Turning back to the stove, the woman bustled about as she stirred a pot of gravy and checked the roast beef. Eva seemed to have been forgotten. And she figured maybe it was for the best.

As she faced the door, Cody's piercing screams

continued, filling the entire house. No wonder Miss Mamie had called in the doctor. Every evening it was the same. The baby cried and cried.

Clamping an iron will on her fears, Eva pulled off her apron, set it on the sideboard, lifted her head in determination and walked into the other room. Down the hall leading to the back bedrooms, she followed the baby's plaintive cries. And when she reached the doorway to his nursery, she stood there feeling lost and all alone in the world.

Wearing only his diaper, Cody lay on the changing table with Tyler leaning over to inspect him. The doctor moved a stethoscope over the baby's perfectly formed miniature chest and abdomen. Cody kicked his tiny legs, closed his eyes, scrunched up his face and howled in outrage. Yet Tyler seemed completely unruffled by all the fuss.

"There now, little guy. It's okay. We'll wrap you up in your blanket in just a moment." Tyler smiled and spoke in a soothing voice.

Mamie Stillwater stood beside the doctor, her dark, flashing eyes filled with concern. At the age of seventy-eight, Mamie was the matriarch of the Stillwater family. A woman with an iron will and a delicate bone structure who had withstood the test of time. Her cottony white hair couldn't diminish the regal beauty she'd carried throughout her life. But just now she was clasping her wrinkled hands in frustration.

"He sure is mad, Dr. Grainger. No matter what I do, I can't get him to stop crying," Mamie said.

Tyler cooed and spoke gently, trying to calm the angry baby. "I think he's just colicky. See how he pulls his legs up toward his stomach? Crying at this time of the evening is normal for a baby of his age. It'll pass soon enough. Just be patient."

Eva listened intently, feeling lulled by the deep bass of Tyler's voice. Since he was a pediatrician, he must know lots about kids that Eva had never even contemplated. But since Little Horn was such a small town, Eva had heard that he also treated an adult patient on occasion.

"Oh, I'd forgotten about colic," Mamie said. "No wonder he's upset. It's been so long since I had a small baby to care for. I don't know what I'll do if I don't soon find a nanny to help take care of him."

Eva's heart pinched hard. Watching the red, squalling baby wave his thin arms in the air brought out her compassion. She wanted to do something to help him. To soothe him. But fear kept her frozen in place. Babies were her one taboo.

"Any news yet on who the baby's mama is?" Tyler asked as he used a lit instrument to peer into Cody's nose and ears.

Mamie barely spared Eva a glance. "No, nothing since Ben found him on our doorstep with nothing more than a blanket to tell us his name. If only Ben hadn't had that horrible accident right afterward. And now he's lying in the hospital in a coma."

Mamie spoke above the wailing of the baby. The elderly woman sounded so miserable that Eva stepped over and wrapped her arms around Mamie's slender shoulders in a quick hug. "Don't worry, Aunt Mamie. I'm sure Ben will come out of it soon."

"Oh, Eva, I hope so," Mamie said, patting her hand. "I'm so glad you're here. You're such a comfort to me."

Tyler motioned toward a clean terry-cloth onesie sitting on the dresser. Eva quickly handed it to him and he smiled his thanks. She felt charmed.

"Eva, would you mind dressing Cody while I talk to the doctor for a few minutes?" Mamie asked her.

The woman didn't wait for Eva's consent before turning her back and continuing her dialogue. Tyler flashed another smile as he handed Eva the sleeper, then stepped over to the doorway with Mamie. The baby continued to cry.

"You think Cody will be okay, then?" Mamie asked the doctor.

"I do. Nothing to worry about. He's a healthy little boy."

Mamie released a deep sigh. "If only I could find a nanny for him. I'm not used to these late-night feedings. And the constant crying has gotten on my nerves. I feel plumb tuckered out with it all."

Trying not to listen in, Eva slipped the baby's legs and arms into the body suit and snapped it up in front. The poor little dear had cried so much that his voice sounded hoarse. Keeping her hand on Cody's chest so he wouldn't roll off the table, Eva reached for a receiving blanket. No doubt he wanted to be cuddled.

"Last night I didn't even hear Cody wake up until he was screaming his head off," Mamie said. "The child might starve to death with no one but me to take care of him. I'm just an old woman now. Not much use to anyone, especially a young baby."

Tyler chuckled and squeezed Mamie's arm. "That's

not true. Your family loves you. And I'm sure Cody will be just fine. Did you get the results from the paternity test back yet?"

Mamie nodded. "Yes, he's definitely a Stillwater. My great-grandson. I'm delighted, but I sure wish Grady was here and Ben was out of the hospital. Until both men are home safe, we won't be able to figure out which one of them is Cody's daddy."

Ben and Grady were identical twins. Grady was currently serving in Afghanistan on some hush-hush special-ops mission. No one seemed to know where he was or how they could get in touch with him to let him know about the baby and his brother being in a coma.

"I'm sure Grady will check in with you soon," Tyler said.

The crying stopped abruptly, and both Tyler and Mamie turned to look at Eva. She felt their gazes resting on her like a ten-ton sledge. The sudden quiet was unnerving to all of them. Especially Eva. Because she'd done something unthinkable. The one thing she'd vowed never to do. She'd wrapped the baby up in his blanket, clasped him close against her heart and sang him a soft lullaby.

Tyler stared as Eva rocked the baby gently. The child stared up at her with wide eyes, seeming enraptured by her. She was singing softly, her voice high and sweet. A song Tyler remembered hearing his own mother sing on more than one occasion.

He couldn't take his eyes off Eva. Long strands of her red hair swept past her shoulder and she tucked them back behind her ear. Afternoon sunlight streamed through the window, glinting off her auburn highlights. With her pristine skin and soft brown eyes, her profile looked delicate and petite. In fact, he couldn't remember ever seeing a more beautiful woman.

"Why, Eva, I had no idea you knew how to calm an angry baby," Miss Mamie said.

Eva looked up, her eyes filled with wary amazement. "I didn't know it, either. I haven't held a baby since I was a teenager."

Mamie pursed her lips and gave a nod of satisfaction. "Well, that's settled, then. We need a nanny, and you fit the bill. You're hired."

Eva's mouth dropped open in stunned surprise. "What? But I…I can't."

"Of course you can," Mamie said.

The baby began to fuss, and Eva started rocking again, back and forth. Cody immediately quieted. And something about her standing there snuggling the baby close against her chest pulled at Tyler's heartstrings. Her delicate white hands looked so small and fragile against the blue blanket, yet so gentle and loving.

"You're just what Cody needs. I can't think of a better fit." Mamie touched Tyler's arm. "Come on, Dr. Grainger. I'll walk you out."

Before Eva could argue, Mamie turned and led Tyler toward the door. He reached for his hat and medical bag, carrying them in his left hand. Miss Mamie took his right arm, talking nonstop about Ben and Grady and how thrilled she was to have a new great-grandchild.

Tyler vaguely listened, his thoughts on Eva. She hadn't said much, but he'd read volumes in her silence. Looking back over his shoulder, he saw her face flush pink. Her eyes looked wide and wary beneath her thick dark lashes. Her slender body vibrated with nervous energy. If he hadn't known better, he would have said she was absolutely terrified by the thought of caring for the baby. Surely that was his imagination running wild. She was obviously a natural. And aside from crying in the evenings, Cody was an adorable little baby. But Tyler got the impression that Eva didn't want to be anywhere near the child. He could see it in her tensed shoulders, in the way her gaze followed him to the door in an uncertain look of desperation. He had an overpowering urge to comfort her. To tell her she was doing fine and everything would be okay.

Ah, what was he thinking? Other than serving as the baby's pediatrician, he didn't want to get involved. He'd graduated high school with Ben and Grady Stillwater. They'd all been good friends, playing sports together, competing on the rodeo circuit. But Eva was a different matter entirely.

She was several years younger than he was. The twins' tag-along cousin. In the past, Tyler had thought of her as nothing more than a baby sister. A nuisance he'd helped watch out for. After all, she'd been gangly and freckled and too silly for him to take seriously. Now for the first time, he saw her with different eyes. The years had matured her into a lovely woman he couldn't ignore, no matter how much his heart still ached over his own recent loss.

Carrying the baby, Eva followed them outside and stood on the wide wraparound porch. Tyler had heard about her fiancé leaving her at the altar six months earlier. The whole town had been abuzz about it, but no one seemed to know why it'd happened. Eva apparently hadn't said a word about it to anyone. They all assumed her fiancé had got cold feet. Or they'd had a fight. Or they'd realized they weren't really in love. Lots of possible reasons, but Tyler wasn't one to judge. After all, he'd been dumped himself, right before he'd moved to Little Horn a year earlier. His fiancée hadn't wanted him to come here. She'd refused to understand that he had obligations and promises to keep. The local Lone Star Cowboy League had given him a hefty scholarship to go to medical school. In return he'd pledged to open a medical practice here for at least one year. It was a matter of honor for Tyler. Right or wrong, he'd given them his word and he couldn't break it. Even if it meant losing the woman he'd planned to marry.

"Well, thanks for coming out," Mamie said finally.

He inclined his head. "Anytime. I'm on call night or day."

Mamie nodded and went back inside. Eva stood there holding the baby. Cody released a soft sigh of contentment, then made little sucking sounds with his rosebud lips.

Tyler met Eva's eyes. A look of loss covered her face. A look of reluctant acceptance. As if she realized, whether she liked it or not, that Cody had chosen her. And she couldn't turn her back on him no matter what.

"You gonna be okay?" Tyler asked her.

"Just dandy," she said in a crisp tone.

Tyler almost smiled. He liked her spunk. She'd always been determined to do whatever he and her cousins did, sometimes with disastrous results. With no mother or siblings of her own, she'd clung to Ben and Grady like a little sister. And they'd let her. Because she was family. Because they loved her like their own.

Placing his hat on his head, Tyler stepped off the porch. "I'll check back with you in a day or two to make sure Cody's doing all right."

She took a hesitant step toward him, as though she didn't want him to leave. "Yes, please do."

He caught a note of anxiety in her voice. She looked so sad and vulnerable, as though she wanted to be anywhere but here. But surely he imagined it. Most mature women loved holding a tiny baby. But not Eva. Not right now.

"Good night, then." Tipping the brim of his hat, he crossed the yard and climbed into his truck, turned the key and put the vehicle into gear. As he pulled out of the gravel driveway, he knew one thing for sure. Eva did not want to be Cody's nanny. And Tyler couldn't help wondering why.

Chapter Two

Eva didn't sleep much that night. Aunt Mamie helped her move her things into the bedroom adjoining the nursery, but she tossed and turned, fretting that she wouldn't hear the baby if he woke up. But she did, her eyes popping open wide the moment he began to fuss. Snatching up her bathrobe, she skedaddled for his room.

Peering at him in the darkness, she took a deep breath and tried to settle her nerves. Okay. What should she do first? His diaper. He might be wet and need changing. She hadn't done it before, but no big deal. With only a small lamp to see what she was doing, she retrieved a disposable diaper, then copied what she'd watched her aunt Mamie do on numerous occasions. Everything went fine until the plastic tabs got stuck on her fingers. She fought with them for a moment, finally getting the diaper sealed in the right place. Hmm. Not bad.

Until she picked up the baby and the diaper fell off. Eva groaned and tried again. Cody just cooed at her and waved his arms, as though cheering her on. Finally she got the thing attached so it would stay put.

Once Cody was re-dressed she carried him to the kitchen. They'd installed little green night-lights in the hallways so they didn't have to turn on every light in the house and wake up everyone. Martha Rose said the baby would go back to sleep easier if he didn't have lots of stimuli.

Padding barefoot across the cool tiled floor, Eva opened the refrigerator and squinted at the bright light. She snatched out a bottle and quickly shut the door. Thankfully, Martha Rose had made up several bottles before bed. All Eva had to do was warm up one. A simple task for anyone but her. What if she got it too hot or too cold? She'd never done this before and felt mighty uncertain. Concentrating, she tried to remember what Martha Rose had told her to do.

"A pan of hot water," she said to Cody, moving about the dark room with ease.

Balancing the baby with one arm, she worked fast, setting the bottle in the pan of hot water and waiting several minutes while she rocked Cody and sang to him. Aunt Mamie had showed her how to test some drops of milk on her wrist to make sure the temperature was just right. But Eva's hands shook as she picked up the bottle and offered it to little Cody. He latched on to it ferociously and she jerked in surprise. Then she chuckled.

"You sure are hungry, aren't you, little man?" she said softly.

She walked back to his room and sat in the comfy gliding chair. He sucked greedily as she rocked him in the dim light. She hummed a lullaby, trying not to stare at his adorable chubby cheeks. But she couldn't resist. He was the cutest, sweetest thing she'd ever seen.

Toward the end of the bottle he fell asleep and she placed him in his crib. As she stared down at his cherubic face, she couldn't help feeling proud of her accomplishment. Nor could she fight off a feeling of absolute love as it pulsed over her in shocking waves. She'd do anything to protect this innocent baby. Anything to keep him safe. She'd promised herself never to love another man. If she didn't love, she couldn't be hurt. But she'd already broken that vow. And there was no sense in trying to fight it. Because she loved little Cody Stillwater like her own.

After walking back to her room, she curled beneath the warm covers, feeling happy and satisfied. Maybe if she couldn't have kids of her own she could love other people's children. Maybe she could do this job after all.

Early the next morning she wasn't so sure. She was awakened by Cody's cries. Within moments she'd pulled on her fluffy bathrobe and was standing beside his crib. Seeing her, he waved his little arms and smiled, effectively melting her heart.

"Good morning, sweetheart. Did you sleep well…?"

The question died on Eva's lips. She stared. And swallowed hard. Reaching down, she flipped Cody's downy blanket aside. He panted happily, completely oblivious that anything was wrong. But a horrified gasp erupted from Eva's throat.

A rash, bright red and hot to the touch, covered

the baby's face. A quick inspection of his tiny body told her it went no further. Just his cheeks. What a relief. But she must have done something wrong. Something bad.

A gush of panic rose in her throat, bringing with it a deluge of memories. Costly mistakes she'd made recently that had taken hours of work and lots of money to repair. But Cody wasn't a broken piece of equipment or a ruined batch of bread dough. He was a human being. A little innocent person who was depending on her to take care of him. Making an error with him could be catastrophic.

She held out her hands as if to offer reassurance. "Okay, sweetheart. Don't worry. We can fix this. I'll take you to the doctor. Give me just a minute to get dressed."

She scrambled for the doorway, hurrying to pull on her clothes. She splashed water on her face, ran a toothbrush around in her mouth, then jerked a brush through her long, tangled hair.

Back in Cody's room, she saw that he lay completely at ease, his sparkling brown eyes wide and curious. As though he had absolutely no idea that he had a problem. No doubt he'd get hungry before long. Eva raced to the kitchen and warmed up another bottle for him. Through the window she saw that the sun was barely peeking over the eastern hills. A bit early to go calling on the doctor, but she couldn't wait. Cody was too important to her.

No one else in the house was up yet. Eva scrawled a hasty note for Aunt Mamie, then secured Cody in his car seat and scurried with him out the front door to her truck. Correction. Ben's truck. The one he'd said she could use while she lived at Stillwater Ranch.

It took her five minutes to get the car seat buckled in tight. She couldn't figure out the contraption and wished she had a user's guide handy. Finally it clicked into place.

The truck engine roared as she started it. The tires spit gravel as she peeled out of the wide driveway. She tapped the brake, trying to control her speed. An accident wouldn't help anyone.

She barely noticed the beautiful autumn morning. Russet-brown leaves were scattered across the dirt road. The sun painted the eastern horizon with streams of pink and gold haze and glimmered against the short field grass. Herds of Black Angus cattle grazed lazily on the stubby pasture lands. The crisp morning air smelled of hay and horses. Nothing seemed amiss in the world. Yet Eva's hands were shaking like aspen leaves in the wind.

Think. What might have caused Cody's rash? What if she'd done something wrong when she'd put him down for the night? What if she'd used too much lotion after his bath? Or fed him too much milk? It could be anything. She had no idea. Only that she had to get the baby over to Tyler. And fast.

It took fifteen minutes to drive to Tyler's place. Thankfully the Grainger ranch was close by. Only now did Eva realize she should have called first, to ensure he wasn't in town making early rounds at the hospital. She was happy to see his blue truck parked out front.

She glanced at the yellow frame house with white

trim and an overhanging porch. A modest red barn stood off to the side. Rows of boxwoods edged one corner of the house. A pretty fall wreath hung on the front door, ornately decorated with grape twigs and leaves of burnt orange, red and yellow. Tidy flower beds trailed the serpentine walk path. Everything neat and in its place. Not surprising considering how fastidious Tyler was with everything he did. But Eva figured the wreath was his mother's doing.

After hopping out of the truck, Eva hurried around to the passenger side, unclicked the seat belt from Cody's car seat and lifted him out. She folded the blanket over his head, instinctively knowing the cool morning air was too much for his little lungs.

When she turned to go inside, she froze. Tyler stood beside the house. Their gazes met across the expanse of the yard. He was dressed in his work clothes and holding the handle of a bucket. As though he'd just been heading out to do his morning chores before working in his medical office.

She scurried over to him. "Oh, Tyler. I'm so glad you're here."

"Eva. What's wrong?" He set down the bucket and reached out a hand to clasp her arm. His eyes creased with concern as he met her gaze.

"It's the baby. Something's wrong with him. I don't know what I've done, but it's bad. Please help him."

Tyler indicated the house. "Come inside and I'll take a look."

Clutching the baby close against her chest, she hurried along as he led the way. Just hearing his calm, steady voice brought Eva a modicum of comfort.

Knowing he was near made her think all would be well. He'd know what to do. He'd take care of Cody. Tyler could do anything. And after what she'd been through with her fiancé, she was surprised at how much she trusted this man she'd known all her life.

As he led her inside she thought how foolish she'd been to accept this new assignment as a nanny. She should have said no. Last night when Tyler had asked if she was okay, she should have told him the truth.

No. I can't have children, and I don't want to take care of an adorable baby because he's a constant reminder of what I can never have.

Instead, she'd shut her mouth, the words stuck in the back of her throat. She didn't want to confide anything to Tyler Grainger. Or any man, for that matter. The emotional cost was too high. Better to keep her deficiencies to herself. But now she had a real problem on her hands. Cody was sick. What if he had a fever? She had no idea even how to check for that. And she realized just how unprepared she was to be taking care of a young child. A combination of guilt and fear heated her face. She was in way over her head.

Tyler led her into the living area. It was a comfortable room with tall potted plants, two recliners, a sofa, throw pillows and pictures of his family. One photo in particular caught her eye. It showed Tyler and his sister, Jenny, on horseback. The picture was taken from the side. Tyler sat in front holding the reins. Jenny sat behind her older brother, her arms wrapped around his waist, her cheek pressed against his back, her face smiling with absolute adoration. Eva knew the entire family had been heartbroken when Jenny had died years earlier at the age of ten. A real tragedy.

"Come in here," Tyler said.

Eva stepped into an examination room, complete with chairs and a wide, padded table.

Tyler washed his hands in a small sink. Then without asking permission, he scooped Cody from her arms and set him down on the table. His big, strong hands seemed infinitely gentle as he folded the blankets back to take a look. Cody latched on to one of Tyler's large fingers and tried to pull it to his mouth. Tyler gently pulled free of Cody's grasp. The baby sucked his own tiny fist, babbling and kicking his legs. He seemed completely oblivious that anything was wrong.

Eva's heart pounded in her ears. Sweat broke out on her palms. Tyler reached for a stethoscope, then listened to the baby's heart and lungs. Next he took Cody's temperature.

"His temp is slightly elevated, but nothing that alarms me," Tyler said without looking up.

Eva stood beside him, her gaze pinned on Cody as she gripped the edge of the table. "But what about the rash? What caused it?"

"We'll see." Tyler continued his examination. He lifted the baby's arms, then checked his ears and mouth.

"Aha! Has Cody been drooling more than usual and chewing on things?" Tyler asked.

Eva shook her head. "I have no idea. I was just put in charge of him last night."

She'd heard of babies drooling, but figured it was

done all the time. And they chewed on everything, didn't they?

"Well, I think I've found the problem," Tyler said with a laugh.

Eva leaned closer, nearly beside herself with worry. "What is it?"

"Cody is teething."

"What?"

He gently opened the baby's mouth and pointed at his bottom gum line. "See there how the gum is red and inflamed?"

"Yes." She stared with rapt attention, wondering how that could cause a rash on the baby's cheeks.

"And see that little ridge of white?"

She stooped forward, catching Tyler's scent. A mixture of spice and soap. Pleasant and masculine. "What is it?"

"A central incisor," he said.

She stared at the erupting tooth as if it were something from outer space. "But isn't he too young to be getting teeth already?"

Tyler shrugged. "Yes, he is. Normally, babies get their bottom central incisors at six months, but some babies start teething earlier. It appears that Cody is in that situation."

There was so much she had yet to learn. So much she didn't know. "Will it harm him?"

"Not at all. But once the tooth comes in, you'll want to start brushing it with a soft bristled toothbrush on a regular basis."

Oh, goodness. She'd had no idea.

Tyler stepped away, letting her dress Cody while

he washed his hands again. She could barely snap up
the baby's sleeper, her hands were shaking so badly.
She'd been scared out of her wits. Fearful that she'd
done something to cause the rash. And once more she
wondered if she was insane to agree to work as Cody's
nanny.

Tyler dried his hands on a paper towel. "I think
Cody is just fine."

"But what about the rash on his face? What's causing that?" Eva asked.

"No one really knows what causes it. It could be
that the baby is rubbing at his mouth an extra amount
and spreading saliva across his cheeks. That would
definitely cause a rash. But it's harmless enough."

He turned just as Eva looked up, her face pale and
creased with relief.

"Well, that's good, isn't it?" She blinked, sending a
large teardrop scurrying down her cheek. She turned
away, wiping at her eyes.

Tyler's heart gave a powerful squeeze. He stepped
close and touched her arm. She glanced at him, looking embarrassed and worried at the same time.

"Eva, don't cry. The baby's fine." He placed a finger beneath her chin and lifted gently, forcing her to
meet his eyes. "Were you really that worried about
Cody?"

Her lips trembled and she nodded. "I thought…I
thought I'd done something wrong. I don't know anything about babies. What if something bad happens
and I don't know what to do?"

Her voice cracked and so did his heart. She'd always been tenderhearted, even when they were little kids. She'd yell at the boys when they'd try to chase a cat. Or make them get down from a tree so they wouldn't disturb a nest of sparrows. Her gentle kindness was one reason Tyler had always liked her so much. Maybe Eva couldn't cook, but she was awfully sweet.

"No, Eva. You'll be okay. You've done nothing wrong. Babies get rashes all the time. But you did the right thing by bringing him to me. I can rule out a lot of problems." He withdrew his hand, still feeling the warmth of her skin against his fingertip.

"Like what kinds of problems?" she asked.

"Oh, roseola and scarlet fever. Those are more serious problems that can cause a rash, which I don't believe Cody has. I think he's just teething early."

She bowed her head over the baby and wrapped him in his blanket. "How can I know if he's got something seriously wrong?"

Tyler leaned his hip against the table and folded his arms. "Fever is a good warning sign. If Cody feels hotter than normal, if he's extra fussy. Things like that are good indicators that something's wrong."

"Well, now that you mention it, he does spit up an awful lot. I worry that he's not getting enough formula. I don't know why they made me his nanny. I don't know the first thing about taking care of him."

He laughed, trying to ease her mind. Trying to soothe her nerves. "Yeah, babies are hard to read sometimes. But I guarantee this little guy is getting plenty to eat. He's strong and healthy. You're doing fine with him."

Obviously he'd been right in thinking Eva didn't want to take care of the baby. Now he realized it was probably due to her lack of knowledge about caring for a young child. So maybe he could help ease her mind. It was what he loved doing, after all. Helping children. But it was even more than that for him. It was his life mission to help save kids' lives. The whole reason he'd become a pediatrician in the first place. Because he'd lost his baby sister when she was only ten years old.

"But why is he spitting up so much?" Eva asked.

He shrugged. "Babies spit up. It takes their little bodies time to adjust to the acid reflux. They burp and it comes up their esophagus. They aren't good at controlling it yet. By about nine months, Cody will stop spitting up all the time."

She released a deep exhalation. "Oh, good. I had no idea." She pointed at Cody's nose and chin. "But what about these tiny white bumps? Is that a different kind of rash?"

He barely had to glance at the baby's face to know what she was talking about. "That's called *milia*, and it's normal, too. It'll disappear within a few weeks. In the meantime, just wash Cody's face with mild soap and water, and the rash should clear up soon."

Another exhalation of relief rushed past Eva's lips. She seemed much more relaxed now that she was no longer worried about the baby.

"Be aware that he may get diaper rash, too," Tyler said.

Eva looked horrified. "I've heard about that. What can I do?"

Tyler quickly explained and discussed what she

should do. He even gave her a tube of ointment with zinc oxide to use in case she needed it. And seeing her fearful eyes, he discussed bath time, immunizations and feeding schedules. Everything he could think of that might help ease her mind. And when they finished their in-depth discussion, she looked a little less worried.

"How's Miss Mamie doing?" he finally asked.

Eva smiled. "Fine, I think. She loves this little guy."

"She's not getting too tired out, is she?"

A new baby could be exciting, but Mamie wasn't a young woman anymore. And Tyler knew she also was worried about Ben being in a coma and Grady stationed in a war zone in Afghanistan. As a doctor, Tyler was concerned that the elderly lady might be overdoing things.

Eva flashed a half smile, which made her brown eyes gleam. Wow, she sure was pretty. A natural, earthy beauty that didn't require the enhancement of makeup.

"I think she feels better now that I'm Cody's nanny. She should have gotten a good night's sleep at least," Eva said.

"Good. I'm glad to hear that."

"I understand you're returning to Austin right after Thanksgiving," she said.

He nodded. "Yeah, that's right."

"Are you going to be practicing medicine there?"

Another nod. "I've kept my condominium there and plan to practice with a co-op of other pediatricians. I'll be a junior partner for a few years, but I hope to move up eventually."

She shuddered. "I don't know how you can stand to live in such a large city. I'd be lost there."

Yeah, he could see how a sweet, gentle woman such as Eva would feel lost without the wide-open country around her. And he liked that about her, too.

"Living in the city has its perks," he said.

"Like what?"

He shrugged. "There's a lot to do there. I enjoy the action of city life. You can't get any of that here in Little Horn."

"True. But we've got the most beautiful sunsets you ever saw." Her voice sounded impassioned.

He hadn't thought about that. In fact, maybe he'd taken the beauty of the rolling hills and open fields for granted. But when he'd left for college he'd fallen in love with the arts, culture and the many conveniences city life provided. He was eager to return.

"I've also got my work," he said. "My partners and I have been approved for a grant from the Food and Drug Administration. We'll be doing research on children's immunizations. I'm excited to be a part of that."

"Well, we'll miss you," she said. "People need a pediatric doctor in this town, and we'll be sad to see you go."

"I won't be gone forever. I'll still be coming home now and then for holidays and such," he said.

He smiled, but inside he felt a bit sad. He'd been practicing medicine in Little Horn for almost a year now. Once he left, the townsfolk would be forced to travel to a larger city for a pediatrician. But he couldn't let that stop his plans.

"Won't you miss your mom?" Eva asked.

"Yeah, but we'll still see each other now and then."

He hoped. He'd asked his mother to move to Austin with him, but she'd refused, saying this was her home and she'd never leave. He hoped his practice wouldn't become so busy that he'd have difficulty getting time off work to come and visit her. But he had to go. It was his childhood dream to practice medicine in the city. It was all he'd thought about for the past year. Returning to his old life in Austin. Picking up his practice where he'd left off. And if he didn't return, it could jeopardize the grant he and his partners had received from the FDA. But he doubted he'd ever find another woman to love. He couldn't trust himself to that kind of heartache again.

"If my parents were still alive, nothing could drag me away from Little Horn," Eva said, her eyes a bit wistful.

"Yeah, you were way too young to lose your folks," he said.

He thought about Eva living out at Stillwater Ranch and was happy she had some family to rely on. He still had his mom, but Eva had no one except for her cousins and Aunt Mamie. Eva had known a lot of loss, just like he had. Both of them had been dumped by their fiancés. Both of them had suffered broken hearts. In a way, they had a lot in common.

"What do I owe you?" she asked, reaching for her purse.

He raised his hand. "It's on the house. I didn't do anything, really. And Miss Mamie paid me plenty yesterday."

She lifted the baby, holding him close against her shoulder before she kissed his downy head. "Well, thank you. I can't tell you how relieved I feel. I so appreciate your help."

He smiled, drawn to her easy, honest manners. She seemed so genuine. So real and down-to-earth. Nothing contrived at all. Not like Kayla, his former fiancée.

"Come on. I'll walk you out," he said.

Carrying the baby, Eva preceded him through the house and out to the front porch. Tyler followed, breathing deeply the fragrance of her fresh, coconut-scented hair. As she walked, her hair swayed against her back like a long, red waterfall. He felt the urge to reach out and run his fingers through the silken length of it, but resisted.

Shaking his head, he tried to clear his mind of such nonsense. The last thing he needed right now was a romantic entanglement.

As he stepped out on the front porch, he slid his hands into his pockets.

"Tyler! Oh, Tyler!"

He glanced over at the barn. Veola Grainger stood in front of the wide double doors. His mother. An early riser, she'd dressed in her blue jeans and boots to help him with some chores before he drove into town to make his rounds at the regional medical hospital. Just now she was waving frantically to get his attention.

"Excuse me one moment, will you?" With a nod to Eva, he stepped off the porch and hurried toward his mom. Eva stood easily within hearing distance.

"Applejack is gone," Veola said, her voice shrill with urgency.

He tilted his head. "What do you mean, she's gone?"

"She's gone, and so is your sister's saddle." Mom's voice rose to a plaintive cry.

A blaze of dread scorched Tyler's skin. Without another word, he ran into the barn and looked around. Morning sunlight streamed through the open doorway. He caught the musty smell of straw and ammonia. Bullet, their sorrel gelding, stood in his stall swishing his tail. But sure enough, Applejack was gone; the mare's stall stood wide-open and vacant. At first Tyler thought maybe he'd left the gate open last night and the mare had wandered off. But no. He distinctly remembered closing the barn door securely, because he'd pinched his thumb in the process. Someone had entered the barn and opened Applejack's stall.

His heart plummeted. Was it possible they'd become the victims of a crime? He'd heard about the cattle rustlings and equipment thefts going on in their community. But he'd never dreamed the thieves might steal his little sister's mare.

He walked back out into the sunshine, feeling heartsick and furious by this turn of events. Eva stood beside her truck with his mother. Mom was cooing and admiring the baby, but glanced his way, awaiting his verdict.

"She's gone, all right," he said.

"You think someone stole her?" Mom asked.

He looked out at the wide-open fields surrounding them, his gaze searching the area for some sign of the mare. "Unless she got loose and wandered off."

Mom shook her head. "No, when I went out to the barn this morning, the doors were closed. She couldn't have gotten out by herself."

"And I guarantee she didn't take the saddle with her," he said.

"But why would anyone steal our mare? That horse is almost twenty-one years old."

Tyler shrugged, trying not to show his anger in front of Eva. "I have no idea. But what surprises me more is that the thieves left Bullet behind. I don't understand why they'd take an old horse like Applejack, but leave the younger gelding."

He spoke calmly. After his father's death he'd learned to be the man of the house, and that had taught him patience and self-control over his emotions. He had to be strong for his mother's sake. Though Mom hadn't said so, he knew she was dreading his return to Austin in four weeks. And Eva was worried enough about baby Cody. With their own problems to cope with, neither woman needed to see him act out right now.

"What would they want with Applejack?" Mom asked.

"I have no idea. She's too old to make a good saddle horse anymore. The thieves couldn't get much for her unless they sold her for slaughter," he said.

Eva gave a small cry of anguish. "They still do that?"

Tyler nodded. "While they don't use the horse meat

here in the United States, they can definitely sell it to foreign countries."

Veola cringed in horror and clasped a hand to her mouth. "Oh, Tyler. That sweet little mare. Jenny loved that horse so much. I promised her that Applejack would live out her days here on the ranch. You don't think the thieves would sell your sister's horse to a soap factory, do you?"

A sick feeling settled in his gut. He glanced at Eva. Her mouth dropped open and her eyes mirrored the outrage he was feeling inside. He thought about the horse thieves and wondered if they knew just how much they had hurt the people they'd stolen from. Applejack wasn't just a saddle horse to Tyler and his mother. She was a beloved member of their family. A sweet reminder of a happier time when his sister had been alive and joyfully riding around this ranch.

"I sure hope not. I'll go call the sheriff right now," he said.

"I won't keep you, then. I'm sorry about this. I hope you find your horse," Eva said, her eyes filled with compassion and sincerity.

Again Tyler got the impression she was the real deal. Genuine and caring. The kind of woman a man could depend upon to the very end.

"Thanks, Eva." He nodded, then turned to run inside the house.

He was determined to find Applejack before it was too late. Before the thieves sold her to someone who might do her harm. But as Tyler dialed the sheriff's office he couldn't stop thinking about Eva Brooks and her wide, gentle eyes.

Chapter Three

Seven hours later, Eva pulled into the parking lot at the regional medical hospital in town. She killed the engine of Aunt Mamie's car and withdrew the key.

"Thanks for bringing me here to see Ben," Mamie said.

"You're welcome." Eva smiled and tossed a quick glance over her shoulder at the baby. He lay in his car seat in the back, sleeping soundly. His sweet little face warmed her heart.

"I can't believe the difference in him. He's so calm and happy lately. You're good for Cody," Mamie said as she opened her door.

Eva still wasn't convinced. Everything she did for Cody was still so new. She wondered if she'd ever get the hang of it. And it gave her insight into what it felt like to be a new mother. But she felt betrayed by the flush of pleasure her great-aunt's words caused her. She didn't want to be a nanny, but for the first time in her life she thought she might actually be able to do this job. And she had Tyler to thank for that.

She climbed out and retrieved the baby carrier. As she closed the car door, she tried not to jar Cody too much and wake him up. She slipped the diaper bag over her shoulder. With the baby in tow, she took Aunt Mamie's arm and led the woman up the sidewalk to the white brick building.

Little Horn was fortunate to have this nice, new facility. No doubt Tyler had some of his patients admitted here. While she understood his reasons for wanting to return to Austin, she also wished he would stay. This community needed a talented doctor. But Tyler was a bright, glittering star. He deserved the opportunity to shine. And he could do that in Austin with the new research grant he and his partners had received from the FDA.

The automatic double doors whooshed open and they stepped inside. They didn't pause at the reception desk, but headed back to the intensive care unit. The wide, pristine hallway smelled of antiseptic, bacon and eggs. Not a nice combination. A cart stood off to one side, and an orderly was shuttling breakfast trays into the rooms of the patients.

"Good morning." Grace Bingham greeted them at the nurses' station. Wearing a green smock and white pants, she tucked a curl of wavy brown hair behind her ear.

"Hello, Grace. How is my grandson today?" Mamie asked.

The nurse released a short sigh. "The same, I'm afraid."

"Has the doctor been in to see him this morning?" Eva asked.

"Yes, a couple of hours ago. He said there was no change," Grace reiterated.

With her mouth pressed in a stoic smile, Mamie headed into Ben's room. Eva stood by the nurses' station and set the baby carrier on the floor at her feet. From the open doorway, she could see that her cousin Ben lay on the bed, his tall body still as stone. A white bandage had been wrapped around his head. When he'd been bucked off his horse, he'd struck his head on a rock. Now he was hooked up to a variety of tubes and IV drips, to monitor his heartbeat and oxygen level and keep him hydrated. In the dimly lit room, his handsome face looked as pale as the white blankets tucked beneath his arms. His eyes were closed as if he were in a very deep sleep. Mamie sat in a chair beside him and reached up to clasp his hand.

"Hi there, sweetheart. How are you doing today?" the woman said.

She received no response.

"It's so sad," Grace whispered. "He's so blessed to have his family around him."

Eva glanced at the nurse. They were old school friends, so Eva wasn't surprised by the nurse's blunt comment. "Yes, I hope he'll wake up soon."

Ben had always been so talkative and vibrant. Too wild for Eva to keep up with. Grady and Tyler had never approved of Ben's partying. Ben had always been a hard worker, but he played hard, too. And now, seeing her cousin so quiet and unresponsive tore at Eva's heart. She said a silent prayer, asking the Lord to help her cousin recover soon. And to keep Grady safe.

She had to trust God to see them through. This situation was hard on Mamie. It was hard on all of them.

If only Grady were here. He'd know what to do. He was the stoic one. Dutiful and stalwart. They all depended on his wisdom and strength. He'd be able to reassure Aunt Mamie and help them feel better. He'd solve the mystery about baby Cody's parentage, too. Surely he'd know if he'd fathered a child or if it was Ben's baby. But Grady wasn't here, and Eva felt the leaden weight of responsibility resting on her shoulders. She had to take care of Aunt Mamie and Cody with courage and compassion. No matter what her own fears might be, she mustn't let them down.

"Hi, Eva."

She looked up. Tyler stood beside the front desk. And in a fraction of an instant her senses went on high alert.

He'd changed his clothes from when she'd seen him out at his ranch earlier that morning. His blond hair had been slicked back, his face freshly shaved. He wore a white doctor's coat over his blue Western shirt. A stethoscope dangled from around his neck. He must have been making his morning rounds at the hospital. And for some crazy reason she found his presence strangely comforting. He looked good today. Too good.

The sound of boot heels clicking against the tiled floor filled her ears. She looked up. Carson Thorn joined Tyler. Carson was the president of the Lone Star Cowboy League. Eva had no doubt both men had come here to check on Ben's condition.

A buzzer went off down the hall and Grace headed in that direction. "Excuse me, please."

"Hi there." Picking up the baby's car seat and moving him with her, Eva stepped over to greet the two men.

Carson thrust out a hand and smiled as he spoke in a subdued voice. "I came to check on Ben. How is he holding up?"

She shook the man's hand, highly conscious of Tyler standing beside her. Even without looking, she could feel his gaze resting on her. A fissure of awareness swept down her spine. She was suddenly self-conscious about her appearance. Was her hair in place? Did her makeup look nice? She hoped Tyler wouldn't notice the white stain on her coat from where Cody had spit up on her.

"He's doing as well as can be expected, but no improvement," she said.

Carson shook his head. "I'd hoped he would be coming out of it by now. That day he had the accident, he was so upset when he called to tell me he'd found the baby on your doorstep. I should have told him to stay home and I'd drive over to him."

"What happened?" Tyler asked.

Carson shrugged and slung his thumbs through his belt loops. "Ben missed the monthly League meeting. That wasn't like him at all. Especially since he knew we'd be discussing all the cattle rustling and other thefts we've had going on lately. After the meeting ended, he called and told me that he'd found a baby on his doorstep. He was pretty shaken up by it all and wanted to talk. He said he'd ride over to my place, but he never arrived. When I called later on, I found out that he'd gotten bucked off his horse and was lying unconscious here in the hospital."

Tyler shifted his booted feet. "Well, he's getting the best of care. I can guarantee that."

His comforting words brought warmth to Eva's chest.

"Did his doctor say when he should come out of the coma?" Carson asked.

"No, but the longer he's out, the worse his prognosis becomes." Eva spoke softly, not wanting Aunt Mamie to overhear their conversation. It was upsetting enough without scaring the woman any more. The last thing Eva wanted was to make Mamie sick with worry.

"It's in God's hands now," Carson said.

Eva nodded and tried to smile. But under the circumstances she found the situation a bit hopeless and sad.

"Yes, we need to have faith. God will carry us through," she said, determined to believe her own words.

Tyler made a low, derogatory sound in the back of his throat. He looked away and she got the impression he didn't agree. That wasn't so strange when she considered that she hadn't seen him in church since he was a teenager. As a kid he'd always attended with his parents, but not anymore. And she couldn't help wondering what might have changed him.

"Any news about your missing horse?" Eva asked Tyler.

He shook his head. "No, but the sheriff's working on it."

"I think the league's Rustling Investigation Team should pay a visit to your place, just to have a look around. They might be able to figure out who stole your horse and saddle," Carson said.

A hard glint filled Tyler's eyes. "I'll take any help I can get. In fact, I'd like to become a member of the team and help with the investigation, too."

Carson blinked in surprise. "But aren't you leaving town soon?"

"Yes, but does that matter?" Tyler asked.

"I guess not, but I didn't think you'd be interested," Carson replied.

"Well, I am. I'd like to help out until it's time for me to leave, if that's okay. I want to catch the thief as bad as anyone else. And I want my mare back, too."

Eva caught a hint of anger in his voice. She knew Tyler was upset about losing his horse, but she didn't think he had time to join the league in its investigations. No doubt having his mare stolen had incentivized Tyler to get involved. The situation had become personal to him. Yet she detected something deeper within his motives. She just had no idea what that might be.

"Okay, I think we can arrange for you to become a member of the investigation team," Carson said.

"Good. I'd appreciate it." Tyler forced himself to speak in a calm voice.

Recovering his sister's stolen horse meant a lot to him and his mother. The theft was a deep invasion into their private lives. Knowing that someone had sneaked into their barn late at night while they were sleeping made both him and Mom feel violated. It also made him furious. As though he'd let his baby sister down again. He hadn't been able to save her life back when she'd got sick, but he sure as shootin' wanted to get her horse back. He'd promised her that he'd look after Applejack. That the mare would live out her days in comfort. Not become fodder for the slaughterhouses. He had to keep his word. He had to recover the mare. And he didn't want to share his personal reasons with anyone else.

"I'd like to help with the investigation, too," Eva said.

Both men stared at her in astonishment.

"But why?" Carson asked.

She inclined her head toward Ben. "I've got one cousin in a coma and the other one is in Afghanistan fighting a war. With a new baby to take care of, Aunt Mamie has a lot on her mind right now. She doesn't need to worry about thieves, too. She needs my help to look after the ranch. I'm trying to take some burdens off her. I'm all she's got right now. It's the least I can do for my family. So, I want to help."

The baby made a little squealing sound. They all looked down as Cody squirmed, stretched and yawned. His little eyelids fluttered open and he looked up at the adults standing around him. Eva swung the car seat back and forth in a gentle rocking motion to quiet him. Tyler watched her, thinking her jaunty movements were adorable. In spite of her misgivings, she really was quite good at caring for a child.

"His rash looks a little bit better already," Tyler observed.

She nodded with satisfaction. "Yes, thanks to you."

He flashed a wide smile, unable to help himself. Her words brought a joyful fullness to his chest. For some reason this woman's opinion mattered a great deal to him. When he'd come here to check on Ben, he hadn't expected to see Eva, too. But being near her caused his heartbeat to speed up.

"You sure you want to join the investigation team, Eva? They'll be traveling around to visit various theft sites, and you've got this little guy to look after." Carson gestured toward the baby.

"Yes, I'm sure. I'm not trained in investigation work, but I can sure be vigilant and ask a lot of questions. And Cody won't be any trouble. He's a good traveler and he sleeps most of the time anyway," she insisted.

Carson nodded. "All right, then. I'll make the necessary arrangements."

She gave a decisive nod. "Thank you."

Carson bent down to smile and touch the baby's hand. Cody promptly latched on to the man's finger and Carson laughed.

"He's got a strong grip, but my hands aren't very clean," he said.

Eva beamed with pleasure and Tyler could hardly take his eyes off her.

"When are you returning to Austin?" Carson asked.

It took Tyler a moment to realize the man was speaking to him. He jerked his gaze away from Eva, feeling embarrassed to be caught staring at her. "Um, I'm scheduled to leave the day after Thanksgiving."

But now Tyler wasn't so sure. He didn't want to leave his mother until he'd recovered his sister's horse. That might take some time. Mom already was upset that he was going away, because she'd be all alone. Until this year she'd let most of their land lie fallow and hadn't been running any livestock. This summer, Tyler had worked hard to get the ranch back in shape…just in time to leave again. And Mom wasn't thrilled by the proposition. She didn't say a lot, but he could tell by the sad, faraway look in her eyes that she didn't want him to go. But he had to. Had to get out of this dinky little town and back to his old life. He just didn't belong here anymore.

Or did he?

"Well, I better get back to work. If there's anything I can do, you just say the word," Carson told Eva.

She smiled. "Thank you. I appreciate that."

Carson left, and Tyler figured he should do the same. There was no reason to stay here any longer. Yet he liked being near Eva. She had a soothing way about her that made him feel at ease.

"You'll be missed when you leave town," Eva said.

Her words brought a hard lump to his throat. Other than his patients, he figured only his mom would miss him. It was nice to know someone else cared. "Thanks. I appreciate that."

"I can see how you'd rather live in the city," she said.

He caught a bit of hesitancy in her voice.

"But you don't agree?" he said.

She inhaled deeply and let it out, then shook her

head. "Don't get me wrong. I love living at Stillwater Ranch. And I love the twins and Aunt Mamie. But it's not my home. Not really. But Little Horn is. It's the town where I grew up. Where my people are from. It's a part of me. It'll always be my home, no matter where I go."

Tyler swallowed hard. "Yeah, I get that."

And he really did. He was surprised by the difference one event could make in changing his mind-set. Losing his sister's horse had hit him harder than he thought. It had reminded him that this was his home, too. That his mom was counting on him. That he'd been raised in Little Horn. Whether he liked it or not, this community was in his blood.

Eva arched one of her eyebrows. "But you don't agree?"

He released a pent-up breath. "I didn't use to, but maybe now I do."

She inclined her head, her long ponytail bouncing. "What do you mean?"

He looked at the baby, wondering what he should say. "At one time I thought Little Horn was nothing more than a tiny speck on a very large map. A go-nowhere town with a big dead end in front of me. All my life I dreamed of becoming a respected doctor. Living in a city far away from cows and a small-town environment. I wanted the lights and action of a big city. I wanted to do medical research and live anywhere but here."

Oh, maybe he shouldn't have told her all that. But for some reason, Eva was so easy to talk to. He felt as though he could confide his deepest secrets in her. An odd notion, surely.

She took a step closer. "And now?"

He gave a scoffing laugh. "And now I'm not so sure. Losing Applejack has hurt Mom and me a lot."

What an understatement. Losing that horse was agony. Tyler felt torn up inside. As though he'd lost his best friend. And suddenly he felt as if he was a part of this community he'd tried so hard to shun. He had to protect his ranch. But more than that, he had to protect his family. His father had fought so hard to keep their home. Laboring with blood, sweat and tears to build it into a prosperous place to raise his children. Tyler's sister had died way too young, but that didn't change his feelings for the place. He couldn't walk away from his mom and childhood home without making things right. Not without recovering Jenny's horse first.

He realized Eva was partly to blame for making him recognize all of these feelings he'd kept bottled up inside. He needed to get away from her. Fast. Before he made a huge mistake and asked her out.

"I better get going, too. Like Carson said, if there's anything you need, all you have to do is call and I'll be there," Tyler said.

And he meant every word. He wanted to protect Mom and their home. But he felt protective of Eva, too. Maybe it was an offshoot emotion from when he'd been young, riding around Stillwater Ranch with Ben and Grady. He'd always helped them look after their little cousin Eva. But somehow Tyler's feelings had changed toward her recently. Something he couldn't quite put his finger on. He only knew he was worried about her. He cared about her and Miss Mamie. And the baby, too. He wanted to help them out. Yet it was something more. Something he'd never felt before. Something he didn't understand. And that scared him. A lot. Because caring brought with it a lot of heartache. And because he'd vowed never to care for another woman as long as he lived.

Chapter Four

That afternoon Eva pulled up at Grainger Ranch and killed the engine to her truck. She hadn't planned on returning so soon. She'd been here early this morning, yet it seemed like days since she'd made her mad dash to take Cody to visit Tyler. And in that short amount of time, Cody's rash was doing much better. But she'd received a call from Carson Thorn, telling her that the league's Rustling Investigation Team was meeting over at Tyler's place. Since she was now a member, she had to be there, too.

As she looked out the windshield, her heart gave a slight flutter at the thought of seeing Tyler again. For some odd reason, she hadn't been able to get him off her mind and hated that someone had stolen his sister's mare. But she didn't want to think about Tyler, or any man, for that matter. Because the combination of caring for baby Cody and thinking about romance got her yearning for a family of her own. And that would only make her heart ache even worse.

She noticed a variety of cars and trucks parked

in the wide driveway. The sheriff's black-and-white squad car stood out from all the rest. And knowing the reason for it being here made Eva shiver. The thefts going on in their small community were downright creepy. It made her skin crawl to think of all the dishonesty it took to steal from other people, and she was eager to help solve the crimes.

She looked down at Cody, who lay nestled in his car seat, watching her with his big brown eyes. His cheeks weren't quite as red as they'd been earlier, and she was grateful for that. Without any reason whatsoever, he flashed a wide smile and made several cooing sounds. It was as though he were telling her everything would be all right.

"Oh, you little sweetheart." She leaned down and kissed his forehead, then unbuckled him.

His warm baby scent engulfed her. Holding him close against her chest, she opened the door and climbed out. Afternoon sunlight glinted off the eagle weather vane on top of Tyler's barn. The afternoon breeze ruffled the sheets hanging on Veola Grainger's clothesline. Brown stubble dotted the fields surrounding the house, a testament that the hay had been baled and brought in. The land was now at rest for the winter. Tyler had worked hard this year, running his medical practice and farming on the side. He'd been more than busy. And maybe that was why he didn't have a girlfriend. He didn't have time for extracurricular activities.

Worried that the wind might hurt the baby's ears, Eva pulled a blue knit cap over his head. Wrapped snugly in a sweater and blanket, he looked about with interest, his eyes wide and bright. Eva reached back into the truck and retrieved a loaf of pumpkin bread she'd taken from the kitchen at Stillwater Ranch. She caught the sounds of voices coming from the open doors of the barn. A sorrel gelding stood outside, saddled and tied to the hitching post. She headed in that direction. Stepping inside the barn, she paused to let her eyes adjust to the dim interior. She caught the heavy scent of ammonia. Dust motes floated on the air.

"And you noticed your mare missing this morning?" Tom Horton, a member of the investigation team, stood with his back toward the doors.

"Yes, when Mom came out to water the horses," Tyler said.

Eva patted the baby's back, trying not to disturb the group of people. But it didn't matter. Every eye turned toward her and she felt suddenly self-conscious.

"Hi, Eva." Amanda Jones, a woman with short, dark hair, flashed her a welcoming smile.

Sheriff Benson gave her a nod of acknowledgment. And Veola Grainger came right over to see the baby.

"Oh, look at him. Isn't he the sweetest thing?" Tyler's mom said. She reached past the blanket to caress the baby's little hands, her eyes gleaming with adoration.

Cody rewarded the woman with a wide grin.

Everyone laughed, except Sheriff Benson. She was busy snapping photos of the empty horse stall and saddle rack.

"What a happy baby. You sure are good with him," Veola said.

Tyler tipped his steel-gray Stetson back on his head. "That's what I keep telling her."

Conscious of his gaze resting on her, Eva felt her smile falter. She shifted her weight, feeling as though a fist had slammed against her chest. Her breath rushed out in a lung-squeezing sigh.

Tyler stood near the doors, his legs slightly spread, his hands resting on his hips. It was a perfectly masculine stance, strong and in control. And when she looked up and into his dazzling hazel-green eyes, it felt as though a hundred-watt lightbulb had turned on inside her. Despite being in a room filled with people, she felt completely alone with him. "Hi, Eva," he said, his voice soft and low.

"Hi there." A flush of heat swept over her. Her stomach swirled like a merry-go-round.

She tried to ignore him. Not to look at him. But he had a magnetic pull that cranked her gaze right over to him. She knew this man so well. The way his lips tilted up when he smiled. The color of his hair like damp sand on the beach. And the way he always smelled vaguely of spice and peppermint.

Likewise, he'd seen her at her worst. As a scrawny kid with skinned elbows and freckles. The day she'd got bucked off into a cactus bush, he'd helped her get home and had waited with her until her dad arrived. With no mom and her father always working, she'd been pretty much left to her own devices. But she hadn't been afraid when Tyler was there. In those days he'd been like a big brother to her. Always looking after her, always courteous and kind. But suddenly she was seeing him with new eyes. And she didn't understand the emotions thrumming around inside her mind.

She looked away.

"Carson said you'd be joining us. We're glad to have you," Amanda said. "One of the sheriff's two deputies retired last month and she hasn't had time yet to replace him. The other deputy is manning the office in town, so we're a bit shorthanded."

Tom swiveled on his boot heels and gave her a friendly smile that belied his imposing height. "Yeah, we could use another set of eyes."

Their open welcome touched Eva's heart and she gave them a warm smile. "Thank you."

"So, what time did you notice the horse was missing?" Sheriff Lucy Benson, who stood beside Tom, inclined her head to acknowledge Eva's presence, but continued with business as usual. She wore her official uniform, the gold star on her shirtfront gleaming in the dim light.

"That was about five o'clock this morning," Tyler said.

"And you're absolutely positive the mare was here the night before?" Lucy asked.

He nodded. "Yes, she was here when I came in to feed her last night. Everything was closed up tight." He held up his thumb, which showed a small, black spot on the fingernail. "I remember distinctly closing the door because I pinched my thumb in the process. I then received an emergency call from the hospital, so I drove into town. But when Mom found the horse gone this morning, the stall door was wide-open, yet the barn doors were closed. Applejack couldn't have gotten outside without help."

"And they stole a saddle, too?" Sheriff Benson asked.

Tyler nodded, pointing at the empty rack. "Yes, my sister's saddle. It sat right there."

The sheriff snapped more pictures.

Everyone stood back, looking over the area for any sign of who might have committed the theft. The lull in conversation brought Tyler's attention over to Eva.

"What you got there?" he asked, gesturing to the loaf of bread.

Eva handed it to him. "It's for you. Pumpkin bread. Homemade."

He sniffed the fragrant bread, encased in a clear plastic bag. "I hope you didn't suffer any more burns when you made it."

She shook her head. "No, no. You can eat this without fear."

He gave her a teasing glance. "You sure about that? I still remember those caramelized onions."

She swatted his shoulder, finding it easy to laugh at the incident now. He'd always teased her, but now it felt more personal. "Of course, silly. I didn't make the bread. Martha Rose did. It's delicious. I've officially resigned from cooking at Stillwater Ranch."

He chuckled and nodded at the baby. "Well, that's probably good, since you've got your hands full taking care of this little guy."

He stepped near and reached for Cody. "May I?"

"Sure." She handed over the baby.

Tyler held Cody in one strong arm. The two of them looked at each other, and then Cody flashed another smile. Tyler laughed.

"Cute baby," Amanda said.

"Adorable," Sheriff Benson agreed. "Let's look outside."

They all headed out toward the back of the barn. Eva followed, walking out into the sunlight. She immediately noticed boot- and hoofprints in the soft dirt, but she had no idea who had made them. She assumed they belonged to Tyler and Applejack, or Tyler's other horse, Bullet.

"This area is undisturbed. I didn't make these tracks." Tyler gestured to a wide area off to the side.

"I don't see any tire tracks. Do you think whoever took Applejack rode her away instead of loading her into a trailer?" Eva asked.

"Yes, I do. You've got a good eye," Tyler said.

Her face heated up like road flares. His praise made her jittery. She wasn't used to someone complimenting her. Especially a handsome man.

Sheriff Benson followed the prints for several feet, then raised her head and gazed at the willows and sedges growing off in the distance. "The tracks lead off toward the creek."

"Yeah, I followed them on Bullet earlier this morning, right after we noticed Apple was missing. But I lost the trail down by the creek," Tyler said.

"I'd like to take a look, too." Sheriff Benson snapped some more pictures, trailing the hoofprints a short ways. She returned a few minutes later, jotting a few scribbles on a little notepad she kept stowed in her shirt pocket.

"Would you like me to diagram the crime scene? I've done it before," Amanda said.

"Yes, please." The sheriff handed her a sketchbook and she went to work.

"Eva, would you like to help me set out the ID tents?" Tom asked. "We need to identify prints that don't seem to belong to Tyler or his mom."

The man held up some yellow ID tents with numbers on them.

"Sure. I'd be glad to help. I can use all the training I can get," Eva said.

A blue pickup truck rumbled down the lane, a stream of dust following in its wake. Even before the vehicle came to a halt in front of the barn, Sheriff Benson released a low groan.

"Great. Just what I need right now," she murmured under her breath.

Eva braced herself. They all recognized the truck and its owner. She helped Tom as Byron McKay, the league's vice president, and also the richest and meanest rancher in the area, got out of the vehicle. A burly man with chilling blue eyes, strawberry blond hair and a rotten temper to match, Byron lumbered toward them in his pricey metal-tipped cowboy boots.

"Afternoon, Mr. McKay," Tyler greeted the man.

Byron grunted, barely sparing Tyler a glance.

"Sheriff Benson, I've been looking all over town for you," Byron said in a booming voice.

"Is that so?" Lucy said.

"Yes. There are an awful lot of people around the area that have been receiving anonymous gifts of livestock and hay. I want them brought in for questioning."

"And why is that?" the sheriff asked.

Byron settled his beefy hands against his heavyset

hips. "To see if they're the ones who are stealing cattle from my ranch. I've lost a lot of beeves lately. And I lost two more horses just two days ago. It's mighty suspicious that some of the struggling ranchers are suddenly able to acquire such nice equipment and expensive horseflesh, don't you think? It couldn't be a coincidence."

Sheriff Benson met the man's steely gaze without flinching. "Maybe it is and maybe it isn't."

"What is that supposed to mean?" he growled.

"They could be completely innocent. The gifts might simply be from a generous benefactor that has absolutely nothing to do with the theft of your livestock."

He snorted. "There's got to be a connection. I want them brought in for questioning. They need to provide alibis for the latest thefts."

"Hmm. You told me that no one at your ranch saw or heard anything suspicious when your horses were stolen two days ago," Lucy said.

"That's right."

"Well, that makes me wonder if your horses might have known the thieves. Maybe we should bring in your ranch hands for questioning, too."

"What? Why, that's ridiculous. Every one of my employees is carefully screened before I hire them. They wouldn't dare steal anything from me," Byron said.

Eva believed what he said. Everyone feared Byron. Even his family members. The whole town knew he'd turned his back on Mac McKay, his own cousin. Mac had been struggling financially for some time. When he lost his ranch and turned to alcohol for solace, Byron hadn't lifted a single finger to help. The saddest part was that when Mac died six months earlier, his teenage daughter, Betsy, had left town and no one had seen or heard from her since.

"Your ranch hands definitely had lots of opportunity to steal the livestock," Amanda said.

"But they know I'd catch them at it and prosecute them to the fullest extent of the law. They wouldn't dare take a chance stealing from me," Byron raged. The baby whimpered and started to fuss. Tyler handed him and the loaf of bread off to his mother. Cuddling the baby close, Veola stepped away, silently shielding Cody from the big, angry man.

Tyler held out a placating hand. "Look, McKay. If the sheriff is going to question the recipients of the gifts, then she ought to question your employees, too. It's just common sense. We don't want to leave any stone unturned. One of your employees might know something."

Byron whirled on Tyler. "It ain't your worry, Doc. Stay out of this and tend to your patients."

Tyler locked his jaw. "It is my concern. I'm a member of the Cowboy League and a member of the investigation team, too. I also had a horse and saddle stolen out of my barn late last night."

"Oh. You did? Well, um," Byron blustered. "Then I guess maybe you're right. But I have no doubt my people will prove to be innocent. They'd never steal from me."

"I'll take care of the interviews just as soon as I'm finished with my work here," Sheriff Benson said, a dark, stoic look on her face.

Without another word, she turned and walked down to the creek, ignoring Byron's fuming glare.

The rest of the investigators tucked into their work, laying out crime-scene rulers and ID tents. Without so much as a farewell, Byron turned and walked back to his truck. Eva held her breath while he got inside and started up the engine. His tires spit gravel as he pressed on the gas to drive away. She was relieved to see him go.

The group soon finished their work. Tom and Amanda headed for their vehicles.

"I'll check back with the sheriff tomorrow morning," Tom promised.

"Yeah, and I'll act as the liaison between the sheriff and our team. I'll give everyone a call to let them know what the sheriff wants us to do," Amanda said.

"Sounds good to me," Tyler said.

Eva watched Amanda and Tom leave. It seemed that Byron had brought a haze of suspicion and doubt with him. It hovered over the group like a fat rain cloud. Eva didn't want to be here anymore either, but she had to retrieve baby Cody before she could go home.

She looked up at the house, where Veola sat on the porch swing with the baby. Maybe she shouldn't have brought Cody here. She'd wanted to join this investigation team, to help out in some small way. But now she wondered if there was anything she could really do. After all, Tom was perfectly capable of laying out ID tents to mark the crime scene. And she didn't like exposing Cody to big, angry men. She was still nervous about doing the right things for the baby and didn't want to ruin it.

"I'm sorry about all of that." Tyler touched her arm.

She knew without asking that he was referring to Byron McKay's blowup. "It's okay. It wasn't your fault."

An electric current zinged up her arm from where he'd touched her skin. The pall of anger evaporated like dew on the grass.

Her gaze sought out the baby again. She should go, gather up Cody and get out of here right now. Before she got any closer to this charming man.

Tyler noticed Eva looking toward the baby. "You're very attentive to him. I meant what I said, you know."

She glanced up. "And what's that?"

"You're good with Cody."

She flashed a smile so bright that it made his stomach tighten. Wow, she sure was pretty.

"I'm not good with many things. I didn't even think I was very good with Cody," she said.

"But you are. You'll make a great mother someday," he said.

Her sparkling eyes dimmed and she looked away. If he hadn't known better, he would think his words had upset her somehow. He gazed at her wind-tossed hair and soft brown eyes. He couldn't help noticing the sad, wistful look of uncertainty creasing her delicate brows.

"I'm sorry. Did I say something wrong?" he asked.

She coughed as though she had something stuck in her throat. "No, it's okay."

"Are you afraid you might get too attached to Cody?" he asked.

She inhaled a sharp breath. "I'm afraid it's already too late for that. I love that little baby. But no one really knows what might happen with him. We don't even know which of my two cousins is his father. His mommy could return and want him back."

That was true. Yet from the uneasy look in her eyes, Tyler thought that something else was bothering her. Something big.

"Why do you suppose the thief left Bullet behind, but took Applejack?" Eva asked.

Tyler shrugged. "Who knows? Maybe they didn't have time to take both horses. It was probably dark. I got home from the hospital pretty late last night. Maybe they heard me drive up and figured they should get out of Dodge while they still had the chance."

When he was a kid they'd had a barn full of saddle horses. Now they had only two. Correction. One horse. Until they got Applejack back.

Stepping over to the hitching post, he patted Bullet's neck. Then he flipped up the stirrup, hooked it over the saddle horn and undid the cinch.

"You've been riding this morning?" she asked.

He nodded. "Yeah, after you left early this morning with Cody, I saddled up Bullet and did some riding, just to take a look around and see if I could spot Applejack."

He lifted the saddle off the horse.

"Can I help?" she asked.

He flashed her a wide smile. "Sure."

He carried the saddle into the barn. When he turned to retrieve the horse blanket, he found Eva standing behind him, holding the blanket in her hands. He took it from her and picked up a currycomb.

Stepping out into the sunshine, he brushed the horse's short coat. Standing beside him, Eva did likewise, helping him groom the animal. He liked the way she took the initiative and they settled into a quiet camaraderie.

"You must really love kids to become a pediatrician," Eva said.

His throat tightened. "I do, but I actually became a doctor in honor of my late sister. I'm the last Grainger in my family. I'd like to continue the line one day."

"Oh, I didn't know. You must have loved your sister a great deal." She smoothed her hand across the horse's shiny neck.

"I did. When we lost her I decided then that I wanted to help save other children's lives, if at all possible."

"That's very noble of you."

He snorted. "I don't feel noble. Most of the time I just give out a lot of immunizations. But every once in a while I get a patient that really needs my help. And that's when I'm glad I became a doctor."

Even after all these years, thinking about his sister twisted his gut into a tight knot. He'd never forget her pale face as she lay silently in the hospital, dying of virulent strep. There had been nothing any of them could do to help her. He was seven years older than Jenny. Her big brother. He'd always looked after her the way he'd tried to look after Eva. And when Jenny had quietly passed away, it had broken all of their hearts. He'd made himself a vow then and there that he'd do everything he could to ensure that it didn't happen to another child in his care. Not if he could help it.

"Being a doctor is a noble profession. Kids need those immunizations to keep them from becoming really sick. What you do is valuable to our entire community," Eva said.

Her words made him feel good about his decision to come here. But now it was time for him to move on. To return to his life in Austin.

"It's definitely been an interesting career so far," he said.

"Did you always want to be a doctor?"

He shrugged. "I never really thought about it until Jenny died. When my dad passed away a year later, I didn't have the money to go to college. That's when the Cowboy League stepped in and gave me a very generous scholarship that covered my living expenses as well as tuition and textbooks."

"That's nice," she said.

"Yeah, I owe the league a lot. If it weren't for them, I never could have gone to a university. Opening a medical office here in Little Horn was the least I could do to repay them."

But he'd just confided too much. Eva was the first person he'd told all of this to. He hadn't even told his mom the real reason he'd become a doctor. And moving to Austin was where he thought he could do the most good with his immunization research. They had better facilities in Austin and he could help make some good advances with the FDA grant.

He thought about the chain of events that had played such a critical role in his life. He'd gone to medical school, graduated at the top of his class, performed his residency in Houston and finally settled in Austin. But before he'd become too entrenched in his own medical practice, he'd had a promise to fulfill. A debt to repay. It'd been inconvenient, to say the least. But now it was done. He'd kept his word to the league.

"It was the right thing to do. I'm glad you came home to practice medicine, if only for a little while. I'm sure the Lord will bless you for your work," she said.

He snorted. "I doubt the Lord will have anything to do with me."

She jerked her head around and gave him a sharp look. "Why do you say that?"

He focused on brushing the horse. "Let's just say the Lord and I don't have a lot to do with each other these days."

She was very quiet for several moments. He could see her out of the corner of his eye studying him with a somber expression.

"I'm sorry to hear that. May I ask why you believe that?" she said.

He shrugged, not wanting to confide all the hurt he was feeling over the deaths of his sister and father, followed by his harsh breakup with Kayla. After all, Eva had suffered losses just as great as his own.

"I don't think God is much interested in me and my family. Otherwise, why did He take Jenny and Dad when they were so young?"

"I don't know all the answers, but I know God has a plan for each of us. You're wrong, Tyler Grainger," Eva said. "God loves all of us. We may not see His plan for our lives, but He knows. It's our duty to be patient and trust in Him. He'll take care of everything for us, if we just have faith."

"Yeah, well, that's fine for you, but not for me. No matter what, it's been fun working here in Little Horn anyway."

It had, but he'd just changed the topic on purpose. He'd learned a lot and enjoyed helping the people of this community. Friends and neighbors he'd known all his life. His old classmates now brought their young children to him, and serving them seemed to fit him so well. Like a comfortable old glove. He liked that Eva understood and supported his decision. But he wanted nothing to do with God. And that was that.

"Now it's time to move on, I suppose," Eva said.

Her words made him shiver. He wondered if he was making the right choice by leaving. He'd always envisioned himself working and living in Austin. Not here in Little Horn. Not this Podunk town, with people who could barely pay his doctor bills. He had a lucrative job waiting for him in Austin. With more opportunities to research and expand his medical knowledge. That was where he wanted to be.

Or was it?

As he looked into Eva's eyes, he realized he'd said too much again.

The sheriff waved from the front lawn. "Hey, Tyler!"

He turned. "Yes?"

"I've got what I need. I'm heading out now. I'll give you a call later."

He raised a hand in farewell. "Okay. Thanks, Sheriff."

Sheriff Benson nodded and headed over to her squad car.

"I don't envy the sheriff her job," Eva said.

He nodded. "Me either. With all the trouble brewing in our community and dealing with people like Byron McKay, she undoubtedly has her hands full."

"Yeah, but she's dedicated. I'm sure she'll find out who's committing the thefts."

He agreed. "I'm sure she will. And heaven help them when it comes time to make restitution."

"Yes. I'd sure hate to be them when they get caught," Eva said.

"Me too."

A hint of a smile tilted her lips and warmed his heart.

"Well, I guess I should be going, too," she said.

"Thanks for coming out here."

She walked up to the house and he followed behind, wishing she could stay a little longer, yet wishing she would go. She'd hit a little too close to home for his comfort, chipping away at the steel wall he'd erected around his heart. And he didn't like that at all.

The porch swing jiggled as his mom stood and handed Eva the baby. "He's such a jolly little soul. I wish I could spend the rest of the day with him."

Eva laughed. "You wouldn't say that if you'd seen

him at three o'clock this morning. Believe me, this little boy has a powerful set of lungs and isn't afraid to use them when he wants something."

Tyler chuckled, remembering Cody's cries out at Stillwater Ranch until Eva had picked him up and sung him a lullaby. And then her frantic expression when she feared she'd done something wrong to make the baby's cheeks bright red with a rash. Tyler was happy to have assuaged her doubts.

He helped her pack the baby into the car seat. And when she turned to say goodbye, Tyler caught her delicate scent.

He inhaled deeply. "Thanks again."

"You're welcome. See you later." She waved her fingers before he closed the truck door.

He stepped back so she could pull out. Mom joined him there, enfolding her arm with his as Eva drove away.

Mom nudged his shoulder. "Eva's a nice gal. The kind to help you find the answers to any problem troubling you. You should ask her out."

Hmm. Tyler had been thinking the same thing. But no. That would be an exercise in futility. He couldn't do that. It wouldn't be fair to him or Eva. He was returning to Austin at the end of the month. The last thing he needed right now was a romantic entanglement to hold him in Little Horn.

Chapter Five

Eva clutched the phone receiver, holding it tight. Elevator music played in her ear. She was on hold for the third time in the past ten minutes.

Standing in the living room at Stillwater Ranch, she drummed her fingers on the armrest of her chair. A dog barked outside and she looked out the wide picture windows. Tyler Grainger pulled his truck into the yard. Bandit, her cousin's cow dog, ran up to meet him.

Tyler hopped out of the truck and leaned down and scratched the dog's ears before stepping onto the porch. Still holding the phone to her ear, Eva opened the front door before he even knocked. It'd been two days since she'd seen him last and his visit surprised her.

"Hi there," he said, jerking the steel-gray Stetson off his head.

She smiled and stepped back, giving him room to walk inside.

"Hello?" a voice on the other line said.

Eva snapped back to her phone call. "Yes, I'm here."

"What can I help you with, ma'am?" the male voice on the other end of the line asked.

Tyler sat down and politely waited for her to finish her phone call. Instead of his white doctor's coat, he wore a denim jacket over his Western shirt. His scuffed cowboy boots told her he must have been working at his ranch.

"I'm trying to get a message to Grady Stillwater. His family has had a number of emergencies that he should be made aware of," she said.

"Yes, Miss Brooks. I have your other messages here already. All five of them. We're doing everything we can to reach him and pass the word along."

"Can I please speak with his commanding officer?" she asked, knowing it was futile.

"I'm afraid he's in a meeting right now, but I'll be sure to give him your messages," the man said.

Eva took a deep breath and let it go. "Yes, please. I'd appreciate that."

"You're welcome. And have a nice day, ma'am."

A very polite brush-off. Eva knew that when Grady had joined the army, he'd basically signed his personal life away for the duration of his enlistment. But she thought he at least had a right to know about his brother and baby Cody.

"Thank you." Eva hung up the phone, her hands trembling.

"Are you still trying to reach Grady?" Tyler said.

She nodded, feeling frustrated by her lack of success. She felt helpless. No one seemed to know how to reach her cousin in Afghanistan. Or if they did know, they weren't being very communicative or accommodating.

"Yes, I've called everyone in the army that I can think of. I'm trying to let Grady know about little Cody and that Ben's in a coma. I was hoping maybe he could come home for Thanksgiving. But no one seems to know how to get in touch with him. It's like he's disappeared off the face of the earth."

Tyler slapped his hat against his solid thigh. "I take it you just tried his commanding officer?"

She nodded. "Yes, with no help whatsoever. I've even tried the Pentagon, but they haven't returned any of my calls yet."

And honestly she doubted they would. If Grady was on a special-ops assignment, they wouldn't do anything to jeopardize that mission.

"I'm sorry, Eva. I know this must be difficult for all of you. How's Miss Mamie holding up?"

"I'm just fine, thank you."

The woman entered the room carrying Cody in her arms. Tyler came quickly to his feet. Upon seeing Tyler, the baby waved his chubby arms and chortled. They all smiled. It was infectious. Eva couldn't seem to help herself. The baby was a cuteness magnet. Whenever he was in the room, everyone lit up with smiles.

Tyler clutched his Stetson in his hands and shifted his weight. Aunt Mamie had that effect on people, too. She commanded respect.

"What brings you to our place this fine afternoon, Dr. Grainger?" Mamie asked.

She handed over the baby to Eva.

"I thought I'd pay a quick house call just to check up on Cody. To see if his rash has cleared up yet," Tyler said.

He arched his head to get a look at the baby's face.

"Hey, the rash is gone. He's doing great," Tyler said.

"Of course he is. Eva takes very good care of him. She keeps him nice and clean," Mamie said.

Eva nodded, feeling delighted that Tyler had noticed. Since she was the baby's primary caregiver, she took pride in knowing she'd got the rash to heal up. It made her happy to be of some service. But she was almost certain that Tyler hadn't come over here for the baby. Not really. So, what was he doing here?

Mamie folded her arms and gazed steadily at both of them. As though they were two young kids who had been caught smooching in the backseat of her car. Finally, she showed a tolerant smile. "Hmm. Are you sure you're not here for some other reason, young man?"

Tyler flushed beet red and Eva would have laughed if the topic hadn't been so uncomfortable. Seeing this mature man filled with discomfiture in front of Aunt Mamie was amusing for so many reasons. Surely Mamie didn't think Tyler had come here to see her. That was absolutely ridiculous. Not only was he leaving in a few short weeks, but neither of them had done anything to indicate they were interested in each other.

Anyway, even if Tyler asked her out, Eva would have to say no. He loved kids. Had even confided to her that that was why he'd become a doctor. He obviously wanted a family of his own someday. To continue the Grainger family line. Which meant he'd want a biological child of his own. And she couldn't oblige him. It was futile even to think about it. Because she cared for him, she couldn't hurt him by offering any false hopes. She couldn't hurt herself with hollow dreams, either. There was no future between her and Tyler.

"Well, you might as well stay for supper," Mamie said. "We're having roast beef. And you know my Martha Rose is the best cook in six counties. It's usually just Eva and me. It'll be nice to have a man in the house again."

"Oh, I...I don't think I can..." Tyler stammered.

"I won't take no for an answer, young man. You'll stay. I can't wait to hear all about your plans for when you move back to Austin. I want to hear why you think it'd be better for you living in that big city instead of staying and practicing medicine here. Now, that's settled." Without another word, Mamie turned and walked toward the back of the house, her regal head held high, her thin shoulders set in a stubborn posture.

Eva and Tyler watched her go, both of their mouths hanging open.

"Well, I guess you're staying for dinner," Eva finally said.

Tyler's eyes widened with amazement. "Yes, I guess I am. But how does she do that?"

"Do what?"

"Politely give orders that we willingly follow."

Eva laughed. "I have absolutely no answer for you. It's a gift, I suppose. Aunt Mamie and Uncle Cody ran Stillwater Ranch for a lot of years. I think she's a tough old bird in spite of her dainty body."

He laughed, too. "I think you're right. Except for my mother, Miss Mamie is the only woman I'm actually afraid of displeasing. Can I use your phone to call my mom and let her know I'll be home later than expected?"

Eva smiled and pointed at the telephone sitting on the table. While he made his call, she took little Cody to put him down for a nap. Alone in the nursery, she changed his diaper like a pro, wrapped him in his blanket and rocked him for several minutes. It gave her a short time to gather her thoughts. To prepare herself for the evening ahead.

Eva had always cared for Tyler. But if she wasn't careful, she realized her feelings could quickly change. Maybe they already had. But she couldn't allow them to go any further. No, sirree. She could never fall for another man. Especially one who would be moving to Austin at the end of the month.

Tyler had told everyone he wanted to check in on the baby. He was just paying a routine house call. But in his heart, he knew it was something more. He wanted to be here. To be around Eva. Even Mom had said as much when he'd called to let her know he'd be having supper at Stillwater Ranch. She'd again advised him to invite Eva on a date. Of course, he'd refused. He would never ask her out. They were nothing more than friends.

Or were they?

He shook his head, determined not to let it go further than that. He had plans, after all. People were counting on him in Austin, and he couldn't let them down, either. Not if he didn't want to endanger their research grant.

He sat in the living room, visiting with Miss Mamie and Eva. And when Martha Rose rang the dinner bell, the three of them congregated in the dining room and sat clustered near the head of the table. Not a large group, but a happy one. Surrounded by bright lights and the delicious aromas of homemade dinner rolls and tender roast beef brisket. They laughed and talked all at once. It reminded him of when his sister had been alive and his family happily had sat down for dinner together almost every night.

Ching. Ching. Ching.

Miss Mamie tapped her dinner fork against her water glass to get their attention.

"I'm so happy to have both of you here with me tonight. I want to welcome our special guest, Dr. Grainger." She met his eyes. "With Ben and Grady both being gone, it's nice to have a man in the house again, Tyler."

He inclined his head, feeling the warmth of family right down to the ends of his steel-tipped boots. "Thank you. It's nice to be here."

"Would you humor an old lady by offering a prayer of thanks for our meal?" she asked.

Tyler froze. He hadn't prayed since the night Jenny had died. He'd been so angry at God that he'd vowed to never pray again. And frankly, he wasn't sure he knew how to do it anymore.

Conscious of Eva sitting next to him, he looked at Mamie. The matriarch of the Stillwater family. She sat so quiet, her diminutive body graceful and still. Her wise eyes stared back at him, crinkling at the corners with an understanding smile.

Eva moved restlessly beside him. He felt her arm brush briefly against his. Felt the warmth of her skin like the scalding blast from a furnace.

"Sure, I'd love to," he said.

No sense in upsetting these two women with his anger at the Lord. Instead, he bowed his head, closed his eyes and asked for God's blessing on the food. He also asked the Lord to help them do what was right for baby Cody. And to see that Grady would come home from Afghanistan safely. That Ben might recover from his coma. And that each of them would have what he or she stood in need of. He finally closed his prayer in Jesus's name and everyone said, "Amen."

"Thank you," Miss Mamie said.

"Yes. That was nice," Eva said.

She handed him the platter of meat. He took two slices and placed them on his plate.

"Have they found your mare yet?" Miss Mamie asked as she sipped from her glass of water.

Tyler shook his head, conscious of Eva listening intently. "No. In fact, the sheriff doesn't have any major leads at this point. She interviewed all of Byron McKay's employees this afternoon to see if they might be possible suspects in the thefts, but they all had alibis."

A low cry came from the back of the house. It escalated quickly to a piercing shriek. Cody must have woken up from his nap.

Eva set her napkin on the table. "I'll get him."

She left and returned momentarily with the baby cuddled close against her heart. She soon offered him a bottle and he lay content within her arms.

Sitting at the table, Eva continued eating while she held the baby. Watching her maneuver her utensils while keeping the baby happy, Tyler thought her quite skilled.

"I hope they catch those cattle thieves soon." Mamie interrupted his thoughts. "All this dishonesty going on in our community is so bothersome."

Tyler nodded, trying to focus on what Miss Mamie was saying. But all he could think about was Eva and her small, gentle hands rocking little Cody.

Eva glanced at him and his pulse skittered against his wrist. She gave him a smile that shot an arrow straight to his heart. He stared into her luminescent eyes. She laughed at the endearing way Cody clutched folds of her shirt in his small hand. Despite the uncertainty that still lived inside him, Tyler was so happy to see her again. He was mesmerized. She was like a long-lost friend he lamented ever losing. His stomach churned and he wondered what on earth was the matter with him.

Soon after he'd consumed a delicious slice of apple pie and vanilla ice cream, Tyler made his excuses.

"I'd better get home now. I need to check in with Mom," he said.

"I'll walk you out," Eva offered.

Miss Mamie just smiled. "Thanks for a delightful evening, son."

"You're welcome."

He scooted back his chair and headed for the door. Eva followed, carrying the baby. She stood on the front porch with him. And seeing her standing there holding the baby in her arms, he wished…

No! He couldn't go there.

"You were awfully quiet at dinner," she said.

"I didn't have much to say."

She chuckled. "Aunt Mamie tends to do most of the talking. I hope we didn't bore you too much."

"No, of course not. I enjoyed myself."

They were both quiet for a moment, each of them lost in their own thoughts.

"I was sorry to hear about your fiancé," he said.

She hesitated. "Yeah, th-thanks."

She stumbled over the words and he thought she must still be hurting inside. He couldn't help wondering what had broken them up.

"I was engaged once myself," he said.

Now, why had he told her that? The words just popped out of his mouth before he could call them back.

She quirked her eyebrows. "I didn't know."

"We broke up right before I returned to Little Horn." He quickly explained what had happened.

"I think you're better off. It's important that you kept your word to the Cowboy League," she said.

He agreed, surprised by her support. And it felt good to share his feelings with someone else.

"Losing my sister, Jenny, hurt too much and I decided I didn't want to ever open myself up to that kind of heartache again. I tried to build a relationship with my fiancée, but that didn't work out either," he said.

"And yet you'd like to have children one day," Eva said.

"Yes, that's true." He looked away, confused by his own emotions. To have children, he'd have to love and trust someone again. "I kind of locked my heart."

Eva lifted the baby to her shoulder and looped the blanket over his head before she rubbed his back. "If that were true, you wouldn't have become a pediatrician with the hope of saving other kids. Nor would you have honored your promise to move back home to serve the community of Little Horn."

Hmm. Tyler hadn't thought about that. And he realized his desire to help went deeper than he'd allowed himself to believe. It'd taken this kindhearted woman to make him realize that. But the reminder caught him off guard and twisted inside his heart.

"When Kayla broke off our engagement, it hurt me more than I realized. I was trying to do what was right, and yet she wouldn't support me in it. I wanted to marry her, but I felt like she betrayed me. I don't want to ever go through that hurt again, either."

"I can understand that. You should turn your sadness over to the Lord," Eva said.

Tyler swallowed. This wasn't what he wanted to hear, but maybe it was what he needed.

"How did you cope after the breakup with your fiancé?" he asked.

She shrugged. "I didn't. For days I bawled my eyes out. But then I found solace in the scriptures. God's word brought me the comfort I couldn't find any-place else."

He snorted and she jerked her head toward him.

"You don't agree?" she asked.

He looked away. "I've already told you that the Lord and I don't get along very well."

"Yes, and I'm surprised by that. You used to come to church all the time with your parents. What changed?"

He coughed to clear his voice, feeling suddenly very lonely inside. "I guess I did. I got so busy with school and then my residency. I came home to visit Mom when I could. I was running all the time. I didn't have any extra time for the Lord in my life."

But it was more than that and he knew it. He'd turned his back on God and wasn't quite sure how to return.

"I figured the Lord didn't really care much about me," he confessed.

"Oh, Tyler. That couldn't be true. He loves you. I'm sure of it. But sometimes it's easy to forget and push Him away."

Was that what he'd done? Pushed God out of his life? Tyler didn't want to confront the issue, because he feared he might not like the answer.

He wasn't surprised by Eva's solid faith. She was a gentle soul. Yet he thought her to be one of the strongest people he knew.

"Doesn't anything ever rattle your faith?" he asked.

She laughed. "Of course. I'm just like everyone else. I have my own trials and grief to deal with."

Yes, she sure did. Each quiet heart was undoubtedly hiding away sorrow that the eye couldn't see. And just because people didn't talk about their troubles didn't mean they didn't have any. It was easy to get caught up in your own woes and forget that other people had difficulties and regrets, too.

"Sometimes I think it's too late to go back," he said.

"No, it's never too late for the Lord. And I know everyone at church would welcome you back with open arms," she said.

Tyler wasn't so sure. It'd been just over a year since Kayla had dumped him. Even after all this time, her rejection still felt like a needle in his heart. And it occurred to him that she'd never loved him at all. Not really. If she had she would have waited for him. She would have been happy that he was a man of honor and tried to keep his word. But since that time he'd used his pain as a way of never being hurt again. To encase his heart in ice.

"I just wish it didn't hurt so much," she said, as though reading his mind.

He raised his eyebrows. "You mean breaking up with your fiancé?"

She nodded, her eyes soft and melancholy.

He gave a croaking laugh. "Yeah, I know what you mean. Kayla made me choose between her and keeping my word."

"But why did you have to choose? Why couldn't you do both?" she asked.

"Exactly. That was my argument all along. But Kayla didn't see it that way."

Eva nodded with understanding. "If she had really loved you, she wouldn't have made you choose. She would have waited for you. She'd want you to keep your word. She'd know that, deep inside, you couldn't be a man worth loving if you lost your honor."

His mouth dropped open in amazement. Eva understood, so why hadn't Kayla been able to grasp this concept? Dear, sweet Eva, who couldn't drive a tractor without tying up the side rake or cook onions without burning them or do a multitude of other tasks very well. But she knew people. She knew how to treat them right. How to help them out. How to be there for them and love and understand them.

A strand of hair had come loose from her long ponytail. He reached up and brushed it back from her cheek. The feel of her soft skin was so warm against his fingertips. His heart pounded. As he stared into her eyes, he couldn't look away. Couldn't move or even breathe. He thought about kissing her. But that would be disastrous.

And this wasn't getting any easier.

"Well, I'd better go." He stepped down off the porch, glad to put some distance between them.

"Good night." She picked up Cody's little hand and waved farewell.

He laughed, thinking she and the baby the most adorable couple he'd ever seen. And as he got into his truck and drove away, Tyler promised himself not to pay any more house calls to Stillwater Ranch without being asked first. He must not forget his well-laid plans. Finish his work here in Little Horn and return to Austin as fast as he could. He needed to stay far away from Eva Brooks and her sad, beautiful smile.

Chapter Six

Eva stood on the front porch, watching the taillights of Tyler's truck fade into the darkness. Bathed in the glow of the porch light, she listened to the chirp of crickets and the lowing of contented cattle. She gazed out at the corrals, seeing the dark shapes of horses as they settled for the night. The soft breeze carried their scent. This was her home now, yet it wasn't. She didn't belong here. Not really. She didn't belong anywhere.

The weather would soon change and she decided to take advantage of the mild evening. Holding the baby close, she sat on the porch swing and rocked him back and forth. She thought about when Tyler had asked about her fiancé. At first she could barely respond. Her thoughts had stuttered to a halt. Her breath had frozen in her throat. She'd known that eventually someone might ask her questions about what had happened between her and Craig. And she'd thought she could handle it. That she was prepared to reply.

She'd been wrong.

Mamie found her there a few moments later. Lost in her thoughts, Eva brushed at her eyes and looked away.

"Is Tyler gone?" Mamie asked.

Eva nodded, wanting to be alone for a while. She had been trying to sort out her muddled feelings with very little success. In fact, she felt miserable.

"You should go out with him, you know?" Mamie said.

"Who?"

Mamie snorted. "Dr. Grainger, that's who. And you know very well who I'm talking about. He's such a nice young man. Absolutely perfect for you."

Eva didn't agree. Tyler loved kids. He was educated, smart and funny. So good at everything he did. The complete opposite of Eva. They weren't perfect for each other for so many reasons.

"Aunt Mamie, he wouldn't want me like this," she cried.

Mamie wrapped her arm around Eva's shoulders and pulled her in close. "Oh, my dear. There, there. Why would you say such a thing?"

Eva blinked her eyes, sending tears tumbling down her cheeks. The stiff lace of Mamie's collar bit into her skin, but she barely noticed. In a croaking voice, she told her aunt the truth. That she couldn't have children.

"Oh, my dear. I remember that horrible injury when you were young. That ornery old bull that gored you. We nearly lost you. I remember your father was beside himself with worry. We all were. But once you were released from the hospital, I didn't know it had cost you so much. Your father never told me," Mamie crooned softly in her ear.

"That's because I begged him not to tell anyone. It's too humiliating. I'm defective."

"Oh, sweet Eva. It's not your fault. It was just an unfortunate accident. And as I recall, your father sold that bull weeks later. He said he wouldn't have such a vicious animal living on his land."

Yes, Eva remembered as if it were yesterday. The absolute terror as the bull had charged and then the screeching pain. She'd tried to run, but hadn't been fast enough. She'd been rushed to the hospital, covered in blood. At first, she'd thought she would die. And then she'd wished she had. But she'd recovered and had been trying to live with the consequences of that fateful day.

"Don't be so sad," Mamie said. "You're such a wonderful girl. You have so much to offer a man. Anyone would be blessed to have you for his wife."

"But I can't have children. I can never have a family or my own home," Eva croaked.

At least, not as long as she didn't have a decent job that would pay the bills. She'd barely been able to support herself on the meager salary she'd made waitressing at Maggie's Coffee Shop. Even if she was able to pay the adoption fees for a child of her own, she couldn't afford formula, diapers and child care. Besides, she would never consider adopting without a husband. Her personal values wouldn't allow it.

Mamie rubbed her frail hands over Eva's shoulders. "Now, you listen to me. There's more to life than children. And one day someone will look at you and it won't matter what you can or can't give them. It won't matter that you can or can't have children. All they'll see is how much they love and adore you. That's the most important thing. And together the two of you will figure out all the rest of what you want in your lives."

Eva drew back and wiped her nose, not believing a single word her aunt said. It sounded so nice, but it didn't work in real life. At least, not in her experience. But, oh, how badly she wanted to believe it.

"You really think so?" Eva said.

Mamie smiled, her wrinkled face lighting up, her eyes sparkling with wisdom Eva could only hope to attain someday. "I know so. And don't forget, there's always adoption. See how much you love little Cody? That's what adoption is like. Your heart doesn't recognize that this baby isn't from your body, does it? Of course not. You love Cody just because he's sweet and wonderful and he needs you. And one day, you'll have children of your own. Even if that means you have to adopt them to have a family. They'll still be yours."

Eva gave a small shudder. She knew she would have no problem with adoption, but it wasn't that way for everyone. It hadn't been that way for Craig. And she wondered how she'd ever find a man who wouldn't begrudge her for not being able to have kids. "I could easily adopt, but my fiancé couldn't do it. At first he said he could, but he changed his mind at the last minute. He told me adoption wasn't the same as having your own kids. That he couldn't accept someone else's brats as his own."

Mamie drew back, her eyes wide. "Brats?"

"Yes, that's what he said. That's why…that's why

he left me at the altar. He just couldn't go through with it after all. He didn't want to be burdened by a barren woman."

"Humph. I'm sorry he hurt you, but I think you're well rid of that fella. You deserve so much better. That's not the kind of man you would want to be with," Mamie said.

Eva agreed. In a way, she'd been relieved that Craig had broken up with her. But now she doubted she'd ever find someone else. Someone she could trust. And if she did, how would she ever truly know that they didn't feel the same way about adoption as Craig?

She let Aunt Mamie hold her for several more moments. She'd grown up without a mother and it felt good to be doted on. Eva wanted to feel solace. To believe what her aunt told her. But all she felt inside was empty desolation.

"I promise you that good things are in store for you, my sweet Eva," Mamie said. "You've just got to have faith in God and be patient. Years from now you'll look back on this time and everything will make sense. It'll all settle into place and you'll know that it happened the right way."

The woman's words sank deep into Eva's heart. It was what she needed to hear right now. What she wanted to cling to and hope for. But marriage was a two-way street. She'd been dumped once. She couldn't go through that again. She'd tried hard to accept that she couldn't have children. That she could never marry and raise a family of her own. But no matter how hard she tried, she couldn't get past the void in her heart.

She hugged her aunt. "Thank you, Aunt Mamie. Thank you so much for being here for me."

"You're welcome, dear."

And in her heart, Eva recommitted herself to having more faith in God. She silently prayed that He would help her get over her craving for a happy marriage and a family. That somehow, the Lord could take these feelings of longing away from her and fill her up with something else. Yes, she wanted to have faith, but she still believed her situation was absolutely hopeless.

On Thursday evening Eva drove Aunt Mamie into town for the monthly league meeting. During the drive, Cody fell asleep in his car seat. Glancing back at the baby, Eva felt calm and domestic. A comfort she hadn't felt since her father was alive.

She pulled into the parking lot outside the nice facility the league had built several years earlier. It was a ranch-house type of building with a wraparound porch, lots of cheery lights and spacious lawns for playing volleyball and other games during the annual Fourth of July party.

As Eva unbuckled Cody's car seat, she glanced up. The sun was setting in the western sky, highlighting the rolling hills that surrounded them with a variety of grays, pinks and blues. It was so beautiful that it made her throat ache. She loved this town. She'd had so many girlhood dreams of living here and raising her children. But instead she'd known only heartache.

They got out of the car and stepped onto the winding walk path.

"Hello." Mamie nodded politely to Frank and Lenora Woods as they headed toward the building.

Frank waved, but Lenora chugged on by, her pointed nose high in the air.

"Well, I wonder what's gotten into her?" Mamie spoke in a low whisper.

Eva reached into the diaper bag for a burp cloth, wiped the drool off Cody's chin, then picked up the car seat. "I wouldn't pay her much mind, Aunt Mamie. She's never been very friendly."

Mamie frowned. "You think it might have something to do with her being on her third marriage?"

Eva shrugged. "Could be. But there's got to be a reason her other marriages didn't last. I'm not in a position to judge, but I'm not sure that Lenora is the easiest person to get along with."

Mamie slung the strap of her purse over her shoulder and closed the car door. "Maybe it's good that she doesn't have any children. It must be difficult living out at that chicken ranch of hers. I know I certainly wouldn't want her for a mother."

Eva didn't agree. Maybe Lenora was like her and couldn't have children. Maybe that was why Lenora had such a sour attitude. They couldn't see it on the outside, but everyone had sorrows and heartaches on the inside that they had to deal with. And Eva was determined not to let her problems decay her like that. But she didn't dwell on the topic long. Her thoughts were preoccupied with the recent thefts in the area and what progress they could make in recovering the missing cattle and horses. Especially the mare that had been stolen out of Tyler's barn.

As they walked up the front steps to the meeting hall, the crisp air smelled of coffee. They filed into the spacious foyer. People stood with their heads together as they greeted one another, laughing and chatting.

Eva looked up, her gaze landing smack-dab on Tyler. He stood at the front of the room talking to Carson Thorn. Dressed in crisp blue jeans, his best cowboy boots, a gray Western shirt and a turquoise bolo tie, Tyler looked nice. His blond hair was slicked back with a bit of gel. No doubt he'd cleaned up before coming into town for the meeting.

His eyes met hers across the room. His handsome mouth curved into a warm smile and he inclined his chin as he listened to something Carson was saying. Then he tilted his head back and laughed. His gaze locked with hers. A buzz of excitement thrummed through her bloodstream. He'd confided a lot to her about his fiancée, and she wasn't sure she wanted to get any closer to him.

The baby started to fuss and she used the opportunity to look away. Mamie took the diaper bag while Eva picked up Cody. The baby instantly quieted. She pulled the knit cap off his little head. His downy hair stood straight up with static electricity. Eva laughed and smoothed it down. He didn't mind. Looking around with wide-eyed curiosity, he seemed happy to have a better view of the world.

"Evenin', Miss Mamie and Eva," Sheriff Lucy Benson greeted them as they passed by.

"Good evening," Mamie replied.

"How's Ben doing?" the sheriff asked in a kind voice.

Mamie sighed. "The same, I'm afraid. There's been no change whatsoever."

The sheriff folded her arms across her starched uniform. "Well, hopefully that'll change soon. Is Grady still overseas?"

"Yes." Mamie jerked her thumb toward Eva. "Eva's tried numerous times to get in touch with him. Until they're both home, I'm trusting the Lord to take care of my two boys."

The sheriff rested a consoling hand on Mamie's arm. "I'm sure He will. I'll keep them in my prayers. And you give Grady my best when you talk to him again."

Mamie showed a sad smile. "I'll do that."

Sheriff Benson slid on past and greeted several other people at the door.

Byron and Eleanor McKay walked in, followed by their two sons, Gareth and Winston. The teenage boys were fraternal twins, tall and good-looking, but everyone knew they had a streak of anger and rebellion in them, just like their father.

Seeing the family, Mamie tugged on Eva's arm. "Let's sit over here."

Smart move. Eva had no desire to speak with Byron, either. Lifting the baby carrier over the tops of chairs, Eva willingly followed her aunt. The woman headed toward a vacant row of seats and they both plopped down to wait. Eva scanned the room, her gaze pausing for several moments on Calvin Pierce. A widower with two teenage daughters to raise, Cal was okay-looking and pleasant enough, but he was quite a bit older than Eva. And honestly, she just wasn't attracted to the man. Not in the least. And even though she didn't think she could be choosy, there was one thing Eva refused to budge on in selecting a marriage partner. No matter what, she would not wed someone she didn't love. Period. And Cal was the only single man she knew who already had kids. But maybe someday, another widower might come along. A good, kind man with kids in need of a mother to love them.

When Tyler joined them moments later, Eva's cheeks flamed hot and her thoughts scattered to the wind.

"Howdy." He smiled, his eyes resting on her.

"Hello." Her voice sounded rather breathless, and she covered it up by shifting the baby to her other shoulder.

"Good evening, Dr. Grainger. Is your mother here tonight?" Mamie replied.

"I'm afraid not. She thought tonight might be rather contentious, so she stayed at home."

"That's probably smart. Won't you sit with us? Maybe you can make sense of all this rustling business for me."

He tilted his head. "I'm not sure I'll be of much help, but I can try."

"Hi, Doc." Caleb Shepherd flashed a wide smile. He sat just in front of them, swiveling around in his seat to chat.

"Howdy. How's Spencer doing?" Tyler asked after the man's four-year-old son.

Everyone knew the little boy had recently suffered

from a bad case of pneumonia. As the only pediatrician in town, Tyler had been the boy's doctor.

"He's doing better, thanks to you. He's slowly getting his energy back and he sleeps through the night again. We've got an appointment with you next week, so we'll bring him in to see you then," Caleb said.

"Good. I'm glad to hear it."

Susan Shepherd lightly tapped Tyler's arm with her fingertips and gave him a look of gratitude. "I don't know what we would have done without you. You saved our little boy's life."

Tyler smiled kindly. "I'm just glad he's gonna be okay."

They talked a few moments more. Then Caleb turned and faced the front of the room. Susan continued to admire little Cody.

"He sure is cute," Susan said.

Tyler sat beside Eva, his arm brushing lightly against hers. As if on cue, her heart rate sped up. In a room full of people, why did he have to sit next to her? But then she reminded herself that Aunt Mamie had invited him. But she couldn't shake off a nervous energy caused by being this close to him.

Mamie leaned forward to speak to Tyler. "Has there been any news about your mare yet?"

"Nothing yet, I'm afraid. Hopefully we'll hear something soon." He looked at Cody. "Mind if I hold him for a while?"

Eva nodded her acquiescence and the man slid his big hands around the baby. Reclining back, Tyler crossed an ankle over his opposite knee and propped the baby on his thigh. Cody smiled big and waved his little arms. Susan laughed at his antics.

"He's a good-natured baby. The poor little guy, abandoned by his mama on the doorstep. He's so fortunate to have you for a nanny," Susan said to Eva.

Eva nodded and felt a glowing warmth deep in her soul. Cody's colic was the reason he'd been so fussy early on, but she liked to believe that he felt happier because of her. For so long she'd wanted to find one thing she was really good at. But why did it have to be motherhood? Discovering that she was good with babies was both a blessing and a curse. Something she didn't understand. With Tyler sitting beside her, she let herself pretend for several moments that they were a real family. That Cody was hers and she was his mom. That she and Tyler were happily...

Clack! Clack! Clack!

Carson smacked a gavel on the podium in front of him. He cleared his throat and put a smile in his voice. "Okay, folks, let's get started."

People scurried to find their seats and everyone faced forward. The room quieted almost immediately. They all stared at him. The board members sat beside him at the long table, their faces stoic as they silently waited. Eva's gaze skimmed over Byron McKay, who was next to Carson. Byron's cheeks were red, his eyes narrowed with disapproval. He looked as mean as a snake, and Eva couldn't help wondering what he had to be so angry about. He had a wife and family and lots of wealth. It just went to show that money couldn't buy happiness.

"I'd like to call this meeting to order. Do I have a

motion to approve our last meeting's minutes?" Carson waited for a motion.

"So moved," Mamie said.

"I second." Dave Burton raised a hand.

"All those in favor?" Carson said.

A round of *ayes* filled the air as the membership voted.

"All those opposed?" Carson glanced around the room expectantly.

No one responded.

"The minutes are approved." Carson clapped his gavel lightly on the podium. "Next, just a bit of information before we hear the reports from our standing committees. Amelia Klondike is sending a sign-up sheet around the room for our annual Thanksgiving buffet. Be sure to sign up to cook a turkey or bring food items, or you can help out with the cleanup afterward," Carson said.

A low hum sounded throughout the room as people digested this bit of information. The holiday dinner was a big deal in this community. Every league member and his or her family would be in attendance. But since Eva couldn't cook, she didn't think there was much she could do except setup and cleanup.

Carson pounded the gavel once more. "To begin, we'll have a report from the Rustling Investigation Team."

Byron McKay snorted and made a derogatory comment. "They sure ain't been making much progress. I don't know why we've even got an investigations team."

Eva felt Tyler tense beside her. Pulling Cody into

the hollow of his arm, he leaned forward, his gaze zeroed in on Byron. Without asking, she knew Tyler didn't approve of the man's comments. Neither did she.

Carson jerked his head toward Byron and met the man's eyes without flinching. Everyone sat as still as statues. No one took so much as a deep breath. From past experience Eva knew Byron was dying to be named league president, but he never could quite get enough votes. She also knew it'd be highly detrimental to the league if Byron was ever put in that office. He'd rule with an iron fist, which was probably why he couldn't get elected.

"During this meeting, everyone will please refrain from commenting without being recognized first," Carson said in a stern voice.

A tense hush fell over the room. Carson was one of the few men in the room with a strong enough temperament to counterbalance Byron. Tyler was another such man. But with him moving back to Austin, he'd never run for office, nor had he expressed interest in such a huge commitment anyway.

Someone handed Tyler a clipboard with the Thanksgiving sign-up sheet attached. Holding Cody in one arm, he quickly scrawled his name beneath the cleanup category. When he passed the list over to Eva, she did likewise, but also added her name to setup. Not because she wanted to be with him, but because it was a logical choice. Aunt Mamie signed up to bring pies and dinner rolls. No doubt she'd have Martha Rose make them for her.

Tom Horton, the chair of the Rustling Investigation

Team, stood and walked to the front of the room. Without giving away any details of their investigation, he presented a brief overview of the work the team was conducting. Eva thought this was wise since the thief could be sitting right there in the room with them.

The thought made her shiver as she looked left and right, considering the ranchers surrounding her. They all looked so innocent. People she'd known all her life. But there was no telling who might be the culprit or why.

Lenora Woods raised her bony hand and stood.

"I'd like to be recognized," she said.

"All right. Go ahead and speak," Carson said.

"Is it true that some of the ranchers in the area are receiving anonymous gifts of livestock and hay?" she asked.

Whispers rippled through the crowd. Several men and women nodded their heads.

"Yes, I believe that's correct," Tom said.

"Well, I'm a poor struggling rancher. Why haven't I received any gifts? Where's my free stuff?" Her voice had risen to a shrill screech.

"Um, I don't know." Tom stared back, appearing dumbstruck.

Lenora held out her hands in a plaintive gesture and gazed at the throng of people. "I work hard. The bad economy has hit me mighty hard. I'd like some free gifts, too. I need the help more than any."

Eva held her breath, bracing for another storm. Everyone knew that back when Mac McKay had still been alive and his daughter, Betsy, had been in town, Lenora had always complained about them, too. Mac hadn't maintained his fences properly and his goats were always escaping onto Lenora's property and making messes. It had been a constant source of contention at these meetings. Now that Mac was gone, it appeared Lenora had something new to whine about.

"You're not the only rancher that's been hit hard. I'd like some free gifts, too," someone else yelled.

The room burst into shouts as several people stood and started pointing fingers, talking all at once.

Carson pounded the gavel, speaking in a growling voice. "Settle down now. We're gonna follow Robert's Rules of Order here. If you want to speak, you've got to be recognized first."

Cody whimpered and squirmed in Tyler's arms. Eva reached out, expecting Tyler to hand him over. Instead, Tyler surprised her when he smiled and stood at the side of the room to rock the baby.

The throng quieted by slow degrees.

Carson faced Lenora. "Mrs. Woods, I can't answer your question. You already know the league isn't responsible for the gifts. We have nothing to do with them, nor do we know who the benefactor might be."

"I think it's Amelia Klondike," Lenora accused with a sneer.

Amelia whirled around, her blond curls dancing.

"Amelia is certainly rich enough to be giving gifts all over town," Lenora continued. "And she's also a do-gooder over at the church. It's got to be her."

Having finished her diatribe, Lenora sat down with a huff and glared her disapproval at Amelia.

Amelia stared wide-eyed with astonishment, her mouth dropping open in surprise. Not only was she the league's events coordinator, but through the local church she also had founded Here to Help, a cluster of community workers who assisted the less fortunate whenever they could. In the past Amelia had been generous with her inherited wealth, and Eva had wondered if she might be responsible for the gifts. But the shocked look on her face said differently.

"Believe me, I wish I could take the credit, but it's not me. I'm not the benefactor," Amelia said.

Lenora scoffed and cynicism laced her tone. "Yeah, do you really expect us to believe you?"

Amelia folded her arms, her jaw set hard. "You can believe what you want, Mrs. Woods, but I didn't give out any of these gifts. I can assure you of that."

Cody continued to fuss, and Tyler bounced him lightly back and forth. Seeing such a big, strong man comforting the cranky baby did something to Eva. She'd expected him to hand back the child as fast as possible, but he just continued to comfort the baby like a real dad would do.

Lenora's face reddened. She obviously didn't like Amelia's response. And Eva wondered if it had been a mistake to come to the meeting tonight. She wanted peace in her life, not contention. She didn't like exposing Cody or herself to this kind of conflict. But with Aunt Mamie sitting in rapt attention and Tyler holding the baby, Eva couldn't easily make an escape and go home. At least, not yet.

Chapter Seven

Tyler lifted Cody up to his shoulder and bent his knees, bouncing the little boy gently. The baby snuffled and rubbed a little hand against his eyes. He obviously was tired. And no doubt the loud voices at the league meeting weren't helping the situation.

When Eva reached over and handed him a pacifier, Tyler smiled his thanks. He pressed the Binky against Cody's mouth and the baby latched on, sucking furiously, his eyes drooping.

Tyler glanced around the room. Amelia sat in somber silence, while Lenora Woods fumed. Tyler didn't think Amelia was the person behind all the anonymous gifts. But if not her, then who? And what criteria did the benefactor use to choose their recipients? Why did they give hay to one family and not to another?

A burly hand lifted into the air and Carson acknowledged the owner. "The chair recognizes Byron McKay."

Byron cleared his gravelly voice. "The investigation team is a good idea, but they've got to accomplish better results."

His tone insinuated that the team was anything but effective.

"What exactly are you saying?" Tom Horton asked.

"Just that we might want to consider new membership on the team," Byron said.

"Oh, yeah. Like who? You? As if you could do any better," Tom scoffed. "We can't go around telling all of you what we're doing, or the rustlers would find out. We can't catch them by exposing our work. We need to keep things quiet until we have some concrete evidence."

The color on Byron's face deepened. "Keeping quiet is just an excuse to hide your incompetence."

"Incompetence? How would you know? You're not a member of the team."

Byron opened his mouth to reply, but Carson interceded with his gavel. They all suffered through another series of pounding on the podium.

"I'll have order in this meeting, or we'll end it right now. You gentlemen are out of order." Carson's eyes hardened and anyone who looked at him could see he wasn't kidding. He would shut down the meeting if everyone didn't behave.

Byron and Tom both clamped their mouths shut, but heavy disapproval filled their eyes. Tension and anger hung so thick in the room that Tyler could have sliced it with a machete.

"We're not changing the team," Carson said. "Tom and Amanda were duly elected for the year. I appointed Tyler and Eva to work on the team, as well.

Per our bylaws I'm within my rights as the league president to do that. They need time to act. It wouldn't be prudent for them to disclose all of their work to this body. But rest assured that they're working with Sheriff Benson to discover the thieves."

Everyone relaxed just a bit and the room seemed to breathe a sigh of relief. With order restored, they addressed various other issues, but the cattle rustling was the high priority. Something had to be done. But what?

Following the meeting, Tyler sat beside Eva and Sheriff Benson, eating a piece of pumpkin pie from the refreshment table. Eva had given Cody a bottle and the baby slept peacefully in her arms. Tiny milk bubbles oozed from his rosebud lips and Eva brushed them away.

"Can you believe that meeting? For a moment there I feared it might erupt into a good old-fashioned brawl," Miss Mamie said, her eyes shining with morbid glee.

"Me too." Eva chuckled, but she looked a bit nervous.

No doubt she hadn't liked the loud voices and arguments. Neither had Tyler. For some reason, he wished she hadn't come here tonight. As a member of the investigation team, it was important for her to be here and participate, but he wished she hadn't witnessed all the anger in the room. He wanted to protect her. To keep her safe. But he wrote it off to their childhood, when he'd felt the same way because she'd had no one else to look after her.

"Carson does a good job of keeping the order," Sheriff Benson said.

"Yes, he does," Eva said.

Tyler set aside his empty plate and fork. "You know, something occurred to me while I was listening to Lenora's complaints tonight."

"And what's that?" the sheriff asked.

"Maybe we should be considering *who* exactly is receiving the anonymous gifts and *who* isn't receiving any. Maybe the people who aren't receiving gifts might innocently know something about who the benefactor might be and why."

Eva shifted the baby slightly, tugging the blanket over his chubby little arms. "You know, you're right. All of the recipients of the gifts have been struggling ranchers. At least they have that in common."

The sheriff nodded. "You're right. I'll get on it. I can create a list of ranchers to compare and consider. Maybe something might jump out at me."

Tyler agreed. "It couldn't hurt."

"Thanks for the suggestion, guys. And now I'll say good-night." Lucy stood and, with one last adoring smile at the baby, stepped away.

"Good night," Eva called after her.

Mamie stifled a yawn with her hand. "Well, this old gal is needing some serious beauty rest. Are you ready to go home?"

She looked at Eva, who nodded. They all stood.

"I'll walk you out," Tyler said.

He waited while Eva buckled the baby in, then snuggled him up nice and warm before pulling on her own coat. He couldn't help watching her care for the baby. The soft smiles, the gentle touches. There was no mistaking that she loved this child.

He picked up the baby carrier, then escorted her out the door, carrying Cody for her. At the last minute, Mamie got tied up in conversation with Nelda Markham, a woman of her age. Eva kept going and Tyler packed the baby out to their car. Eva unlocked the door for him and he set the carrier close by on the sidewalk.

As he lifted the diaper bag inside, two older women were walking by. In the glow of the streetlight, they immediately bent over the sleeping baby.

"Oh, what a cutie-pie. He has his mommy's chin," one woman exclaimed.

"And his daddy's nose," the other woman said. "You must be very proud."

Confusion filled Tyler's mind. They obviously thought he and Eva were the baby's parents.

Eva inhaled a sharp breath. Even in the dim light Tyler could see her face flush beet red with mortification.

"Oh, but we're not… I mean, we aren't…" Eva stammered.

"What's his name?" the first woman asked.

"Cody," Tyler supplied.

"What a perfect name for a perfect baby."

The women smiled with admiration. When they moved over to the sidewalk, he finally exhaled. They were completely oblivious that their words had caused them any discomfort.

He turned to Eva. For a flashing moment, he saw intense misery in her eyes.

"Eva, are you okay?" he asked.

"Yes, I was just thinking about…" She hesitated and gave a sad little laugh. "Oh, it's nothing, really. Just ignore me."

But he knew. All the things she wasn't saying, and he still knew it had something to do with her broken engagement and being left at the altar with no groom.

"Are you thinking about your fiancé?"

She nodded and looked away. "Yes, unfortunately."

"Do you want to talk about it?" He didn't want to push. It was private, after all. But he sensed her need to talk.

A deep scowl creased her forehead, as though she were in pain. "I…I can't have children. And so, he didn't want me anymore."

Tyler stared, his heart thumping madly in his chest. Confusion filled his mind. "I don't understand. You can't…?"

"Have children," she finished for him.

"But how? Why?"

Her eyes shimmered like glass and she swallowed, her slender throat exposed to the cold air. "You remember when I was a girl and that bull charged me? I was in the hospital for two weeks."

He nodded, remembering the horrible incident. They'd all been worried about her. She'd been critical for several days. Her father even thought he might lose her. But then she'd recuperated fast.

"I recovered but not without a price. I can never have children." Her voice sounded strangled, as though she could hardly stand to say the words.

A hard lump settled at the base of his throat. "Oh, Eva. I didn't know."

She shrugged and wiped at her eyes. "It's okay. I haven't told many people. Just you and Aunt Mamie."

He rested a hand on her arm, realizing how difficult it must have been for her to tell him.

"Something like that could make you angry at the world," he said.

She nodded. "Yes, but then I realized that wasn't what God wanted from me. He wants me to be happy."

"You really trust in the Lord, don't you?"

Another nod. "He's all I have left."

Her words touched him deeply. He couldn't believe that she'd trusted him enough to confide in him. To tell him such a deeply personal fact about herself. "I'm sorry, sweetheart. So very sorry."

"Yeah, me too." She showed a half smile that didn't reach her eyes.

"But what about adoption? There are lots of sweet kids in the world that need loving homes to grow up in."

She shrugged. "At first Craig said he'd be willing to adopt, but he changed his mind on our wedding day. At the last minute he realized he wanted his own kids, and I couldn't give him that. So he moved on. I got stranded at the altar with no groom. And that's that."

Her words stabbed his heart. He thought about how he'd feel if someone had done that to him. And then he realized Kayla had done almost the same thing for different reasons. Because he'd come here to Little Horn. But he wondered if he could never father a child of his own, could he accept that? Could he feel as satisfied with adoption?

Yes! The answer came to him as clear as day. In his heart of hearts he knew that he could. Because he already loved the many children he served. Other people's kids. New babies, toddlers and gangly preteens. They each needed a safe place to belong. He loved his patients without reservations. But adoption? Yes, he could do that, too.

"I could adopt so easily," he said with conviction.

She snorted. "Lots of people say that, but when it comes down to it, it's not so easy. Craig said he could adopt. At first. But then after he thought about it, he changed his mind. And then he didn't want me anymore."

Tyler's heart gave a powerful thump. He couldn't imagine giving up on Eva just because she couldn't have children. It wasn't her fault. And it'd be cruel to cast her aside because of it. If she were his fiancée, she'd be his prize. Children were just an expression of the love he would have for her. Nothing would ever take precedence over her. Not for him. Not ever.

Mamie came scurrying out of the meeting hall, zipping her coat as she navigated the serpentine walk path. "I'm sorry to keep you waiting, kids. Nelda wanted Martha Rose's recipe for pickle pie." She leaned closer and spoke in a conspiratorial voice. "But I can't give it to her. Martha Rose would skin me alive if I did."

They all laughed, the tense mood broken. Without a word, Tyler opened the car door for the older woman and waited while she got settled. Before he could close the door, she reached out and touched his hand.

"Thanks for being here for us tonight, dear boy. And you come on out to the ranch anytime. We love seeing you. Don't we, Eva?" Mamie tossed a knowing look toward Eva and waited for her reply.

"Yes, of course we do," Eva agreed, but she didn't meet his eyes. In fact, she looked at the steering wheel, the dashboard, the diaper bag. Anywhere but at him.

Tyler caught the note of hesitancy in her voice. He sensed that he made her nervous. And no wonder. She'd told him something very private. And he'd never betray that confidence. Because she'd trusted him with her secret. All he wanted to do was make it right for her. To take away the pain. And he realized if anyone had a right to hate God and to never fall in love again, it was her.

Eva waited for Tyler to close Aunt Mamie's door. To back away from the car so she could pull out. She had to get out of here right now. Before she burst into tears and melted into a puddle on the road.

She started up the engine. And when he finally closed Aunt Mamie's door, Eva backed out and drove off without a backward glance. Out of her peripheral vision, she saw Tyler raise his hand. Mamie waved, too. But Eva kept on going.

She'd told him too much. She should have kept her mouth shut. But now he knew the truth. He knew everything. Yet she hadn't seen pity in his eyes. No, he'd looked at her with nothing but compassion and kindness.

Glancing in her rearview mirror, she saw him standing right where she'd left him. He hadn't budged an inch. His hands were in his pockets, his broad shoulders hunched against the cold. As though he were still watching over them until they were safely home.

"He's such a nice man," Aunt Mamie said.

"Yes, he is," Eva said.

She couldn't say any more. Because she wholeheartedly agreed. Tyler was nice. A good, strong man who made her wish she dared take a second chance. But that was impossible. And hoping and dreaming for something different would never change the facts. She was finished with men. Finished with opening her heart. Because Tyler deserved more than she could ever give him. He deserved a family of his own. But she was damaged goods. And she wouldn't do herself any favors by hoping for a different outcome.

Chapter Eight

Two days later Eva lifted the crystal vase off the coffee table and set it aside with the lacy doily. She sprayed lemon-scented furniture polish over the oak top and rubbed it with a soft cloth. The chirp of the telephone ringing caught her ear, but she knew Aunt Mamie would get it. She'd just put Cody down for a nap and wanted to finish the dusting before he woke up.

"Eva?"

She looked up. Aunt Mamie stood in the doorway leading to the room they used as an office.

"Dr. Grainger's on the phone for you," Mamie said.

Eva's heart lurched up into her throat. She went very still, wondering why just hearing Tyler's name caused this kind of reaction in her.

She set her cleaning supplies aside and walked into the office. Aunt Mamie handed her the phone, then disappeared down the hall.

Taking a deep breath, Eva spoke into the receiver. "Hello?"

"Hi, Eva. It's Tyler." His voice sounded warm and friendly. Not at all disapproving.

"Yes, what can I do for you?" A fissure of awareness crept up her spine.

"We've had another theft. Over at the Cutters' ranch. The investigation team is meeting the sheriff over there right now. Can you join us?"

She swallowed, tried to speak calmly. After all, she was part of the team. Tyler had called just to let her know what was going on. She considered backing out and resigning from the team, but couldn't do it. She had to face her life. She wasn't going to hide away as though she had something to be ashamed of.

"Of course. I can be there in thirty minutes," she said.

"Good. I'll meet you there."

She hung up, then went into the kitchen to ask Aunt Mamie if she could watch Cody for a couple of hours.

"Of course I can. You just put him down, so he'll sleep through most of it," Mamie said.

Martha Rose showed a huge smile. "Hmm. I don't know how you did it, gal, but you've sure made a difference with that baby."

"Yes, isn't she a wonder?" Mamie agreed.

Eva just smiled, surprised by their respect. She wasn't about to tell them that she'd done very little. He was getting past the cranky stage and had turned into a sweet little boy. She doubted it had anything to do with her.

Martha Rose slid a plate of fresh chocolate chip cookies in front of her and reached for a package of tin foil. "Take these cookies with you. I'm sure the investigation team would like some refreshments."

Eva waited while the woman tore off a piece of foil and wrapped it over top of the cookies. She didn't want to hurt Martha Rose's feelings, but she doubted the team was much interested in refreshments while they investigated a crime. But maybe the Cutters might like them.

"Thank you." Carrying the cookies, she went to check on Cody one last time, then retrieved her coat and purse.

Within minutes she was in her truck and headed over to the Cutter Ranch. When she arrived, the sheriff stood beside Tyler in the front yard. Clark and Jane Cutter stood with them.

"Hi, Eva," Tyler greeted her.

The sheriff barely looked up, busily jotting notes on her clipboard. Clark Cutter was talking fast and gesturing toward the barn.

"We only went to Fort Worth for the weekend. Just a quick trip to see our new grandbaby. When we got home we found that our barn had been broken into," Clark said.

"So, you have no idea when the theft might have occurred?" Lucy asked.

"Yes, it must have been late last night. One of our hired hands used the quad yesterday. He insists he parked it inside the barn, but this morning when we got home it was gone," Jane said.

"Maybe the thief knew you were out of town and your place would be easy pickings. It would take time to steal a four-wheeler and drive it off your place without being seen. But if the thief knew you were gone, they'd have plenty of time for the theft," Eva said.

Jane took a deep breath and let it go. The shock was written across her face. Just like Tyler's mom, Jane looked dazed and violated.

"That's possible," she said. "It's as if the thief knew his way around our place. I can't believe someone we know would do this to us."

"Did people know you were going to be out of town?" Sheriff Benson asked.

"Yes. We talked about the new baby at church last Sunday. All of our friends knew we were making the trip. But who would do such a thing?" Jane cried.

Clark wrapped an arm around his wife's shoulders and pulled her in close. She looked near tears.

"There, honey. Don't worry. We'll catch them," he promised.

"But what if they come back? What if they try to come into our house to rob us? We could be killed in our sleep," the woman whispered in a voice thick with emotion.

Sheriff Benson reached out and squeezed Jane's arm. "I think you're safe enough. This is a thief we're dealing with, not a killer. I don't believe they'd try to harm you."

Jane nodded, but she didn't look convinced. And Eva's heart went out to the woman. What a horrible thing to experience.

"Can you tell me what else was taken?" Sheriff Benson asked.

"Three bridles, two brand-new saddles and a new

chain saw. I hadn't even taken it out of its case yet," Clark said. "I was planning to use it to cut some firewood next week."

Tyler touched Eva's arm and indicated she should follow him. He led her over to the barn doors. "Thanks for coming over here so fast."

"It was no trouble," she said.

"Who's watching Cody?"

"Aunt Mamie. He's down for his nap. Where are Tom and Amanda?" She stepped away from him. His touch was like a zap from a cattle prod, shooting currents of electricity up her arm. It was better if she put some distance between them.

"Tom got delayed and Amanda is out of town for the week. I'll fill Tom in later on."

Like the last time, Eva scanned the dirt for any clues. The sheriff and the Cutters joined them there moments later.

"Look!" Eva pointed at the ground.

She waited while Sheriff Benson reached down with a plastic bag and picked up the item carefully so that she didn't taint any possible fingerprints.

"It's just an old wristwatch," the sheriff said.

They all gathered close and peered at it. A battered watch with a white face and black leather band.

"It's not ours. I can tell you that," Jane said.

The sheriff held it up higher so they could get a closer look. "Are you sure?"

Clark shook his head. "I've never seen that watch before in my life. But I can't tell if it's a man's or a woman's watch."

"Me either," Tyler agreed.

Eva studied the plain watch. "It looks old and like it's been used a lot. But it could be worn by either a male or a female."

"Yes, I agree," Tyler said.

"Hmm. I'll ask around town, to see if it looks familiar to anyone. Maybe that will give us some leads," Sheriff Benson said.

"It might belong to the thief," Eva said.

Tyler nodded. "Good point."

Again, a flush of pleasure swept over Eva. There was no denying that this man had a way of making her feel nice about herself. As if she was valued and could conquer the world.

Tyler took a breath. "Do you think the thief might return tonight hoping to get it back?"

Sheriff Benson nodded. "They might once they notice it's missing. I sure would. To retrieve the evidence."

She slid the watch inside the evidence bag, sealed it, then slipped it into her jacket pocket.

"So, what if we plan a little greeting for them? We could hide out here tonight in case they decide to return for the watch," Tyler said.

The sheriff showed a sly smile and nudged Tyler's shoulder. "You read my mind, Doctor. We could set up a little sting operation to welcome them." She glanced around the yard, at the tall maple trees near the barn and the large tractor sitting off to one side. "There are lots of places we can hide. We wouldn't get much sleep, but we might catch ourselves a thief."

Tyler grinned. "You can count me in."

"And me too," Eva said.

Tyler jerked his head toward her. He frowned and opened his mouth, as if he wanted to say something, but he didn't. And she got the impression he was troubled by something she'd said. She wondered what was going on inside his mind, but figured he'd tell her when the time was right.

"I want to catch this thief," the sheriff said.

Eva agreed. Something hardened inside of her. She wanted to stop this reign of fear. She might not be good at lots of things, but she was honest and hated seeing the look of alarm in Jane Cutter's eyes. And she wanted to help bring the villains to justice.

Like last time, Tyler helped Sheriff Benson lay out crime-scene rulers and ID tents. There wasn't much to go on. There were so many tracks in the dirt it was difficult to tell which had been created by the hired hands and which might have been made by the thief or thieves. With such a small police force they had very little fancy equipment to figure it out. But still, they had to try.

The sheriff showed Eva how to take the necessary pictures of the crime scene. Eva listened eagerly, seeming genuinely interested in helping out. She laughed at something funny Sheriff Benson said and Tyler felt as though he'd been doused by a bucket of ice water. Being near Eva had that impact on him. It woke up his senses every time. And then he thought about what she'd said about faith and wondered if maybe she was right. Maybe he'd turned his back on God. Maybe he should give the Lord a second chance.

"Okay, I think that's it for now," Sheriff Benson announced finally.

They packed up the equipment and Tyler stowed it in the back of Lucy's squad car. When he closed the door, the glint of sunlight caught his eye. Eva held out a plate of goodies to Jane Cutter. Rays of sunshine gleamed against the silver tin foil.

"Martha Rose made these for you. I hope you enjoy them," Eva said.

Clark peeked beneath the foil covering. "Yum. Chocolate chip cookies. My favorite. Thanks, Eva. You tell Martha Rose I said thanks, too."

Eva smiled and Tyler realized she genuinely cared about other people. She had a gift for making people happy.

"See you tonight." Eva waved and headed toward her truck. And that was when Tyler decided he had to say something fast.

He joined her, taking a quick moment to open her door for her. "Let me get that for you."

"Thank you," she said.

She stepped over to climb inside, but he caught her arm, tugging her back. "Eva, I don't want you to come back for the stakeout later on tonight."

She went very still, her expressive eyes showing her confusion. "But why not?"

He hitched one shoulder. "We don't know how dangerous the thieves might be. It could be more than one. I don't want you to get hurt."

All right, he'd said it out loud. He was worried about her. And he told himself that was okay. After all, they were childhood friends. But maybe his concern was a bit over the top.

"I doubt anything bad will happen to me. Besides, the sheriff will be here with us. I can't let the team down," she said.

"But I'd feel better if you were safely at home," he admitted.

She laughed, the sound soft and sweet. She rested a hand against his chest, just below his left shoulder. Her touch was warm and light, and it rocked him to the core. Before he could stop himself, he reached up and closed his hand over hers, squeezing lightly.

"You're worrying needlessly, Tyler. Everything is going to be just fine. And hopefully we'll catch the thief and put this all behind us," she said.

He stepped closer. Eva's mouth dropped open. She took several shallow breaths, her gaze lifting to his. And then something clouded in her eyes. Distrust. A look of pure grief. So wrenching that he knew she must have been thinking about what she'd told him about not being able to have kids. In fact, he realized the secret haunted her. It hung over her everywhere she went.

"Eva." He whispered her name, wishing he could reassure her and that she'd actually believe it didn't matter. Not to him.

She pulled her hand free. "Well, I'd better get going. I'll see you tonight."

She stepped away and climbed up into the truck. He stared after her as she buckled on her seat belt. He opened his mouth to say something else, to beg her not to come tonight, but the words clogged in his throat. He had no idea what he wanted to say. His emotions broiled inside his mind like hot coals. He couldn't think them through.

"Yeah, tonight. You drive safe," he said.

She started up the truck, but she didn't meet his eyes again. She pulled the door closed. Shifting into gear, she pulled out of the yard without a backward glance. He knew, because he watched to see if she would.

Standing in the middle of the driveway, he shook his head. He felt an intense desire to run after her. To tell her it was okay that she couldn't have children. That some good man wouldn't care about that. Not if he really loved her.

She'd had her heart broken. He sensed it every time he was near her. The way she wouldn't quite meet his eyes. Sadness clung to her. As though she felt unworthy of love. And he hated it. Hated that she'd been hurt.

He thought about all the times he'd seen her with Cody. Anyone could tell that the baby brought her complete and absolute joy. She'd make a great mother one day. The kind of mother he'd always wanted for his own children. If he were interested in marriage, of course. Which he wasn't. No, not anymore.

Or at least that was what he kept telling himself.

Chapter Nine

Later that night Tyler returned to the Cutters' ranch.

"Okay, gather around." Lucy Benson waved at him, indicating she was ready to begin their stake-out operation.

Standing in the middle of the barnyard, Tyler joined Eva and Tom Horton. They'd ridden in together in the sheriff's squad car. They didn't want the sight of lots of vehicles parked out front to scare off the thief. The sheriff had parked her car out of sight, inside the Cutters' garage.

The late afternoon sun gleamed across the fields, highlighting hints of red, orange and brown autumn leaves. There was a distinct chill in the air and Tyler was glad he'd worn his heavy winter coat. He thought it would be a long, cold night.

"Are the Cutters going to join us?" he asked.

Sheriff Benson shook her head. "Nope. They're spending the night at the motel in town. Until the thief or thieves are caught, Jane feels too squeamish about staying in her own house now. She's too afraid."

Tyler felt bad for the Cutters' plight. He understood firsthand how horrible it felt to be the victim of this kind of crime. His own mom had suggested they stay in a motel, but he'd convinced her otherwise. Once he left town, he feared she wouldn't feel safe in her own home anymore. And that bothered him intensely. Yet he wasn't sure what to do about it. He couldn't extend his stay. His partners in Austin were already inundated with work and eager for his arrival to start their research project. He had to go. They were counting on him.

"Did all of you read through the training booklet I gave you?" Sheriff Benson looked at each of them in turn.

They all nodded.

"Good. I'm sorry we don't have time to act out some scenarios and go through some training exercises," she said. "Maybe we can do that another time."

"That's okay. I came prepared." Tom opened his heavy coat to reveal a long-barreled handgun.

Tyler cringed, but Eva gasped and stepped back.

"Tom! What's that for?" Sheriff Benson said, pinning him with a glare.

"So we can arrest the thief, of course. I'm just being prepared." He pursed his lips in an expression that said he thought that was obvious.

"I'll take that gun, Tom." Sheriff Benson held out her hand. She showed a tight smile that looked more like a grimace.

"But, Sheriff!"

"No buts. Hand it over. You can have it back after this stakeout is finished."

Tom begrudgingly handed over the gun. "I don't

see why I can't have my own gun. I've been trained on how to fire it."

"That's what I'm afraid of." Sheriff Benson shook her head. "I've told you before I'll be the only one with a gun tonight. None of you are deputized. You're all just observers. Got it?"

Tom reached behind his back and pulled out a pair of handcuffs. "What about these? Is it okay if I have my cuffs?"

"Tom!" Eva exclaimed.

"What?" He showed an innocent expression, as though he saw absolutely nothing wrong with what he was doing.

Tyler would have laughed out loud if Tom hadn't been so serious. But as it stood the sheriff looked ready to yell at the guy. And once more, Tyler realized tonight could be dangerous. Above all else, he was determined to protect Eva.

"If it makes you feel better, you can keep the cuffs. But put them away for now," the sheriff said.

Tom complied happily.

The sheriff inhaled deeply and let it out slowly, obviously trying to maintain her composure. Tyler knew she needed more deputies. Sworn officers who were qualified to assist in this investigation, not a bunch of untrained volunteers who might make things worse. Under the circumstances she was being very patient with them.

"Look, you guys. I want you to remember the law of physics," Sheriff Benson said. "You're not going to act unless you're acted upon first. The only person that's gonna possibly make an arrest tonight is me. I don't want anybody hurt. That's my first priority. You got it?"

"Aw shucks, Sheriff," Tom said, showing a hangdog expression that indicated his great disappointment.

The sheriff threw a warning look at Tom. "I mean it."

He held his hands up. "All right, all right. I got it."

Sheriff Benson glanced at Tyler and Eva. "Is anyone else packing heat right now?"

Eva blinked several times, as if that thought had never entered her mind. Tyler knew many people in Texas owned guns, including himself. But the sheriff already had said they should leave their weapons at home. Obviously he and Eva had taken that order seriously. And Tyler hoped Tom didn't do something foolish. One bad mistake could get someone killed.

Both Tyler and Eva shook their heads.

"You're not going to shoot anyone, are you, Sheriff?" Eva said.

"Not unless I absolutely have to."

Eva frowned, her eyes filled with concern.

Tyler nudged her arm. "Don't worry. The sheriff knows what she's doing. Everything's going to be okay."

Eva gave him a sideways smile, looking a little bit reassured.

"Are there any other weapons I should know about?" the sheriff continued, meeting each of their eyes in turn. "Any knives, batons, stun guns, SAP gloves or other devices you can use to do bodily harm to another person? Or any other items on the no-no list of the training materials I gave to you earlier?"

Tom reached for his belt and withdrew a long knife

encased in a leather sheath. Eva's eyes widened in horror.

The sheriff held out her hand. Tom reluctantly placed the blade on her palm.

"Is that it?" she said.

Tom nodded, hanging his head.

"Okay, good. Now that we've got that over with, let's talk about where we're each going to be stationed tonight," the sheriff said.

"I thought I'd hide over in those bushes." Tom pointed at some low-lying boxwoods that edged the front lawn.

The sheriff pursed her lips and shook her head. "Sorry, Tom. That's not a real good idea. We don't know what to expect tonight. If the thief comes riding into the yard on a four-wheeler, they could drive right over the top of you. You'd end up like a squashed armadillo."

Tom frowned. "Oh, I hadn't thought about that."

The sheriff's lips tightened. She quickly told them each where she wanted them to hide and clarified that they weren't to move unless they absolutely had to.

"Just observe and listen. You could be called on to testify in court, so pay attention to the perpetrator. It'll be dark, but try to notice what they're wearing and doing. Are there any questions?"

No one said a word.

"Good. Let's take up our stations, then."

They headed off, huddling in for the night, prepared for a long wait. Tyler kept looking over to where he knew Eva was hiding. As the sun set, he worried if she was warm enough. If she'd be safe. And fretting over her made him even more uncomfortable. Because it made him think of impossible things. Such as asking her out. And delaying his return to Austin indefinitely. And that wouldn't do either of them any good at all, because he was leaving. He had to go. It was time to get on with his life. And he didn't need a sweet woman from his past to distract him from moving on with his future.

Eva huddled deeper into her warm winter coat. Staring into the darkness, she pulled her hood up over her ears and folded her arms, grateful that she'd had the foresight to bring along a scarf and gloves. All this talk about guns and other weapons had made her mighty nervous. She'd known this was a stakeout, to see if they could identify the thief or thieves, but she'd never thought someone might actually get hurt tonight.

Sitting beneath the footbridge leading toward the woods on the west side of the Cutters' property, she clutched a long, black flashlight in her hand. Before leaving her house, she'd put new batteries in and had tested it. The nights were darker and colder now. If the thieves came her way, she wanted to be able to get a good look at them. But she'd be of little use stopping them. Unlike Tom, she didn't want to take any chances with her life.

A chilling breeze swept past, rustling the leaves that littered the ground around her. She glanced over at the tall elm trees, where she knew Tyler hid within the spindly branches. In the pale moonlight, she could just make out his dark shape. He didn't move at all, but knowing he was there brought her a great deal of comfort.

Tom Horton was stationed behind the tool shed. At first, he'd moved around often and she feared if the thief did show up, they might be alerted to Tom's presence. But as the night deepened, even Tom became silent and Eva wondered if perhaps he'd fallen asleep.

She widened her weary eyes, knowing she mustn't close them. Sheriff Benson was counting on each of them, and Eva didn't want to fail her.

The sheriff had hidden inside the barn, with the wide doors open just a few inches. Since they had no idea what direction the thief might come from, they'd tried to cover the entire area.

The tall mercury-vapor lamp bathed the ground in front of the barn in an eerie blue light. If the thief returned for his lost wristwatch, Eva would see him easily enough. No doubt, the sheriff would catch him. Or her. At this point, the thief could be anybody. And they had no idea how many of them they were dealing with, either.

Looking up at the starry sky overhead, Eva thought about Tyler's request that she not come here tonight. He was worried about her. He didn't want her to get hurt. And his consideration touched her heart like nothing else could. For just a moment she wished things could be different between them.

She shook her head, determined not to think about it. Instead she focused on staying awake. She couldn't tell what time it was or how many hours had passed. Her eyes felt gritty with fatigue. She hadn't been getting much sleep anyway. Not with little Cody waking up a couple of times each night for his feedings. Tyler had told Eva that in another month she could start giving Cody some rice cereal before bedtime. Tyler knew so much about babies. She'd really come to rely on him.

With no sleep, Eva would be mighty tired tomorrow morning. But she figured she could take naps throughout the day with the baby. Her work this evening was too important to shrug off. She was a member of the Rustling Investigation Team and she meant to do her part.

The chilling breeze rushed past and she shivered. A subtle sound reached her ears. Like the rustling of leaves across damp pavement. Yet it was something more.

She narrowed her eyes on the barn doors. A dark shape unfolded there. The figure of a lone person, moving furtively through the night. He sprayed the beam of a flashlight all around the ground, as though searching for something.

Eva bit back a gasp. The thief! He'd obviously returned for the wristwatch.

She readied her own flashlight, prepared for anything. Sheriff Benson had told them to stay put. To not take any unnecessary risks. But a shiver of fear washed over Eva just the same. Talking about this sting operation was one thing, but being here and facing the thief in person was something else.

The barn door crashed open and Sheriff Benson appeared, her flashlight in her left hand, her gun in the other.

"Stop! Police! Hold it right there," she demanded in a powerful voice.

The thief was turned away from the sheriff. Without warning, the person hurled the flashlight, striking Sheriff Benson in the head. She cried out and fell back against the barn before she slumped to the ground. Eva gasped, praying the sheriff wasn't injured badly.

The thief whirled around and ran, heading straight toward Eva. She barely had time to notice Tyler dropping out of the tree. In a split second she realized he was too far away to reach her first. A hard lump rose in Eva's throat. Whether she liked it or not, she was about to meet the thief up close and personal.

Clicking on her flashlight, Eva braced herself. She lunged out of her hiding place and sprayed the beam of light over the thief. In a rush of amazement, she took in the villain's height, weight and clothing, just as the sheriff had taught her to do. Noticing everything she could in those few scant moments before he reached her, but she couldn't make out a face beneath the hood of the jacket.

"Stop!" she yelled and planted her feet beneath her.

The thief kept coming, bulldozing right into her like a linebacker. Eva went flying. The hard ground slammed up to meet her. She landed on her back in the leaves, gasping for breath. Her body ached, the air knocked from her lungs. She rolled, trying to regain her feet, but it was too late. The thief sped on past, pounding across the narrow bridge and sprinting toward the thick cover of the woods beyond. Within moments, they disappeared from view.

"Oh," Eva groaned, trying to sit up. Her body hurt. She could hardly move.

"Eva! Are you all right?"

Tyler knelt beside her. He pulled her into his arms, holding her close for just a moment. Yet it seemed like an eternity. Long enough for her to feel the rapid beat of his heart against her cheek. To feel the solid warmth of his arms around her.

She looked up and their eyes locked. In the moonlight, the world spun away, and in that fraction of time nothing existed but them. She breathed in his masculine scent. Her lips parted in surprise. Strong emotions she couldn't describe crashed over her. What was happening? What was wrong with her?

He kissed her. A swift, gentle caress that made her mind swirl in giddy abandonment.

Without thinking, she lifted a hand and rested it against his chest, just over his heart. She planned to push him away, but her mind betrayed her. Instead, her fingers curled around the soft cambric cloth of his shirt and she pulled him in closer.

"Eva," he whispered as one of his hands threaded through her long hair. "I was so worried about you. Are you all right?"

"Yes, I think so," she breathed.

And then he set her aside and came to his feet. As though he'd realized what he was doing and that it was wrong.

Reaching out a hand, he pulled her up, but stepped back fast. Her thoughts whirled like a cyclone in her head.

"They…they got away. I…I'm sorry, Tyler."

"No, I'm the one who's sorry," he said.

She didn't think they were talking about the thief. No, they were talking about that kiss. Something she still couldn't believe had really happened between them. Surely it had been a figment of her imagination. A dream. Or had it? No, it was real. Gloriously real.

"I never should have let you come here tonight. I knew it wasn't safe," he said.

Oh, dear. What had she been thinking? She'd kissed him, or he'd kissed her. She wasn't sure which. But it was a mistake. A crazy thing for either of them to do. They both had their own reasons for not wanting to get involved. The sheriff might have seen them, or Tom. And then it'd be all over town.

"Hey! Are you two okay?" Sheriff Benson ran up and startled them.

They whirled around in surprise. Eva's gaze lowered to the handgun the sheriff still clutched in her fist and she shivered.

"We're fine. But what about you? Are you all right?" Eva asked.

The woman rubbed her forehead, her face pale in the darkness. A dark smudge ran down to her eye. It looked like blood. "Yeah, he hit me in the head, but I'm fine. It's just a small cut."

"I'm sorry, but he got away." Eva spoke in a shaky voice, thinking Tyler had been right. She never should have come here tonight.

"Hey! What's going on? Did you see the thief?" Tom came running toward them.

In the eerie shadows, his face looked drawn and tired. As though he barely had a clue what had just occurred. With his penchant for heroics, Eva thought maybe it was good that he'd fallen asleep.

"He got away," the sheriff told him.

"Oh, no." He looked around, as if he might be able to catch some sign of the thief.

"Did you get a look at the perpetrator? I never saw his face," the sheriff said to Eva.

She shook her head. "Me either. It was too dark. And he was wearing a hoodie over his head. But he was slim and of average height. Most likely a small man, but it could have been a woman, I suppose. I never got a good look at his face."

"I couldn't see much from my vantage point," Tyler added.

Sheriff Benson exhaled a sigh and showed a troubled frown. "Well, at least it's more information than we had before and no one got hurt. That's the important thing. And we've got his flashlight."

"You think you might get some fingerprints off it?" Eva asked.

"Possibly. He might have been wearing gloves. But we'll sure try," the sheriff said.

Eva glanced at Tyler, grateful for the darkness to shield her flaming cheeks. She'd never forget that kiss. It seemed branded on her brain.

"So, what now?" Tom asked.

"Now?" The sheriff holstered her gun. "Now we go back to the drawing board. I made a list of all the ranchers in the area who have been the victims of thefts recently, and also a list of those struggling ranchers who have been the recipients of anonymous gifts. Three struggling ranchers haven't received any gifts."

Tyler shifted his weight restlessly. "That could just be because it isn't their turn yet."

The sheriff looked his way. "You're right. There seems to be no rhyme or reason to the thefts and gifts. I can't see any connection between them, but I'll bring it up with Carson Thorn first thing tomorrow morning. Right now, I'm going to get in my squad car and drive around the area. Maybe I'll come upon the thief again. Come on. I'll take you all home. I'll call you tomorrow and give you an update."

"First, I'd like to take a look at your head wound," Tyler said.

The sheriff nodded her agreement.

A tremor of fear washed over Eva. She hated the thought of Sheriff Benson using her gun. The thief could be anyone. He or she might go to church with Eva. Or work at the grocery store. Or be one of the hired hands working on any ranch. A friend or a neighbor. Someone Eva knew. It was too creepy to consider.

The sheriff headed toward the garage, her stride strong and determined. Tom accompanied her, but Tyler held back for just a moment. Eva looked up and caught him staring at her as though he could see deep inside her soul, past the barricades she'd erected around her heart and into the secrets she'd hidden there.

"Are you really okay?" he asked.

She nodded, not daring to speak just now. Her entire body trembled. A mixture of panic and inadequacy swirled through her. She tried to slap a hard hand on her emotions, but right now she didn't know what upset her the most. The fact that the thief had knocked her flat on the ground or that Dr. Tyler Grainger had kissed her.

Chapter Ten

Eva stepped into the tool shed and flipped on the overhead light. Dim shadows gathered around the workbench as she searched for what she needed. Without Grady or Ben at Stillwater Ranch to do the work, she'd resigned herself to installing the surveillance cameras by herself. After what had happened at the stakeout several days earlier, she was fighting mad. If a camera system was what it took for her and Aunt Mamie to feel safe in their own home, then so be it. It was just too bad they couldn't install cameras out on the range where the horses and cattle grazed. Rustlers could clean them out. Their ranch manager had put all the hired hands on high alert.

After retrieving a tall ladder, Eva balanced it carefully as she carried it outside to the front and leaned it up against the barn. Morning sunlight streamed across the yard. It had rained in the night and the air carried a musty smell of damp earth. A beautiful, crisp day.

She'd just put Cody down for his nap. If she worked

fast she might be able to get the cameras up before he awoke. But it was not likely. Realistically, this project could take hours to complete. She only hoped it all worked when she was finished.

Walking up to the wraparound porch, she sat on the swing and opened the box of equipment she'd received from the league office two days earlier. It contained everything she needed to install a surveillance system.

"You really think you can do this on your own?" Aunt Mamie said.

Eva jerked around in surprise. "Oh, Aunt Mamie. You startled me."

"Sorry, dear." The elderly woman stood holding an empty laundry basket. She'd been hanging clothes on the line in the backyard and must have just come around to the front of the house.

Eva chuckled. "I know it's a daunting proposition, but I'm certainly going to try."

But doubt filled her mind. She gazed at the eight cameras, a plethora of neatly coiled cables, and input and output connectors. Oh, boy! She was in way over her head. The power and network cables were enough to blow her mind.

Picking up the user's guide, she flipped through it, trying to make sense of the instructions. Without saying a word, she knew she was in deep trouble. If she wasn't careful she could make a real mess of the new equipment very fast.

"You don't need to do this alone, you know?" Mamie said.

"I know." Yet she wanted to. So she could feel

useful. As if she was taking care of Aunt Mamie and Cody during her cousins' absence. Nothing was more important than her family, and she took their well-being very seriously.

She picked up a camera and affixed it to the mount that came with it, trying to figure out how to make it work right. The smell of new plastic parts filled her nose. Maybe she should ask one of the hired hands for their advice. But right now she didn't know whom she could trust.

"I think you need some help, so I called in reinforcements." Aunt Mamie pointed toward the east.

Eva looked up and saw a billow of dust rising along the dirt road. Someone was coming down the lane. Within moments, Tyler's truck pulled into the driveway and Eva groaned.

"Oh, Aunt Mamie. What have you done?" she murmured.

"Why, nothing, dear. The doctor's a fine young man. I still think you should go out with him," the elderly woman said.

Eva barely spared her aunt a glance. She couldn't take her eyes off the truck. "There's no sense in trying to set us up. Have you forgotten that he's leaving town soon?"

Mamie shrugged and wiped one of her hands on the apron she wore around her waist. "So? He could always change his mind and stay right here in Little Horn."

Not likely. Tyler was leaving. And the sooner the better. If this was Aunt Mamie's version of matchmaking, it wasn't going to work.

Tyler parked in front of the house and got out of his truck. Eva gazed at his long legs, so well shaped and masculine. Like always, he wore cowboy boots and a denim jacket that fit his shoulders to perfection. As he walked across the graveled driveway, he moved with the confident swagger of a man who knew what he was doing.

"Howdy, ladies. Beautiful morning, don't you think?" He tugged on the brim of his silver Stetson.

"It certainly is. Thanks for coming out here, Dr. Grainger." Mamie spoke in a cheery tone. She was obviously having way too much fun trying to set Eva up with the handsome doctor.

Tyler's gaze settled on Eva as he stepped up onto the porch. "It's my pleasure."

Eva sat right where she was, her hands resting on the variety of cables and connectors. For one insane moment she wished she'd taken more time with her makeup that day. She'd applied a bit of mascara and blush, then pulled her hair back in a long ponytail. Plain and simple. Her faded blue jeans and old shirt were nothing spectacular. Just another workday. But she shouldn't care what Tyler thought about her appearance anyway.

She lifted her gaze to his face but refused to meet his eyes. She couldn't help recalling the kiss they'd shared the night of the stakeout. It had been so fleeting that it almost didn't bear remembering. Yet it had been branded on her mind.

"You've got plenty of your own work to keep you busy. You didn't need to come out here," she said.

He removed his hat. Several strands of short blond

hair curled against his ears. "Sure I did. I can't have Grady and Ben thinking I didn't look after their family while they were out of commission. I know if the situation was reversed, they'd sure do the same thing for me."

True. And his words reminded Eva that she wasn't alone. Not really. Most people in this town helped each other out. But lately Eva thought it might be a false sense of security. Because someone was causing trouble. Someone was stealing from their neighbors. And Eva figured it was just a matter of time before the sheriff figured out who it was.

"Well, I'll leave you two to your work, then." Aunt Mamie stepped inside the house without a backward glance. The screen door clapped closed behind her.

Eva's gaze followed her aunt with misgivings.

"I should have known Aunt Mamie might do something like this. But really, you don't need to stay. I've got all of this under control," Eva said.

As if on cue the camera she'd been working with dropped off its mounting pedestal and thudded on the floor.

Tyler stepped over and scooped it up in his strong hands. "I've already installed the same system over at my ranch. So, really, it's no trouble. Scoot over."

He waved her over on the swing and sat down beside her. She scrunched her knees together, trying not to let her leg touch his. His presence rattled her nerves. She wondered how he could act so calm and collected. As if nothing had happened between them. And that was when she realized that their kiss might not have meant anything to him. Maybe he wasn't as impacted by her as she was by him.

He peered into the box. "May I?"

Resigned to accepting his help, she nodded. He reached for the user's guide. She handed it over, relieved to have his help. She hadn't seen Tyler for three whole days. Thankfully, they'd had no more thefts in that period of time. But another rancher had found bales of hay in his barn last night, with no idea as to where the gift had come from or who had put it there.

She indicated the user's guide. "From what I gather, the first thing we should do is determine where to hang the cameras. They need to be placed strategically around the entrances to the barn, corrals and stable. Any area where thieves might try to gain access."

"Yes, that's right," he said.

She showed him a map she'd drawn of the ranch and where she thought the cameras ought to be placed.

He studied the diagram, then nodded. "I can see you've put a lot of thought into this. I think you're right in line with where the cameras should go. If I get up on the ladder to install the mounting pedestals, do you want to supervise my work?"

He looked at her, his face so close that she could have reached out and caressed his smooth cheek. That was what she wanted to do, but she resisted the urge with all her might. He was freshly shaved and smelled of a hint of spicy cologne. So handsome sitting beside her in the early morning sunlight.

She looked away. "Sure. I can do that."

She moved the box aside and would have stood, but he caught her hand in his.

"Eva."

She stared at their entwined fingers, her feelings a riot of unease. She tried to inhale, but her breath froze in her chest. No, no. She couldn't do this. Not ever again. She mustn't.

"Yes?" she said, her voice a small croak.

"Eva, about the other night…"

She pulled her hand away. "Yeah, how about if we never talk about that again? Okay?"

He hesitated. "Okay, it's just that I…"

She held up a hand. "Really, it's okay. Just forget about it."

He frowned, his voice low and husky. "Are we just gonna pretend that I didn't kiss you? That it never happened?"

Yes! Her mind screamed. That would be the smartest thing they could do.

"I…um, I think that's best."

She ignored the intensity of his eyes, but she felt compelled. Her gaze clashed then locked with his. She couldn't look away to save her life.

"I'm sorry if I made you feel uncomfortable. That was never my intention," he said.

"Yeah, me either."

"It just happened," he said.

She forced herself to ignore the way his hazel-green eyes lit up every time he looked at her. "Yes, and that's why we should forget about it, okay?"

As if that was ever going to happen. But she had to try.

He hiked his eyebrows at that. "Yeah, if that's what you want."

No, it wasn't, but she hoped that he'd take the hint. Part of her said to throw herself into his arms and never let go. But the other part knew the price of giving her heart too freely. It would hurt so much when he rejected her. And she wasn't about to have that happen ever again.

"Still friends?" He showed an endearing smile.

How could she resist him? She couldn't. Not ever.

"Of course," she said.

"Good. Are you going to the investigation team meeting later this afternoon?" he asked.

"Yes." She nodded, barely trusting her voice anymore.

"Do you want to ride into town with me?"

Yes, but it wouldn't be wise. "I can take my own vehicle."

He shrugged and reached for the electric screwdriver. "There's no need. Since I'm already here, I'm happy to drive you in. I'll probably still be working on the camera system when it's time for us to go."

He stood as if that was settled. But it wasn't. Not in Eva's mind, anyway. Not the kiss or the drive into town or the fidgety way he made her feel every time she was anywhere near him. There wasn't anything she could do about it now. Except pray he got out of town soon. And that her heart would still be intact when he left.

This was a mistake. Tyler never should have come out to Stillwater Ranch. When Miss Mamie had called him last night, he should have told her he couldn't help with the surveillance system. But that was a lie.

And it also wasn't neighborly. No matter what his personal feelings might be, he could never abandon a plea for help. Nor could he forget what had led to his awkward confusion.

A kiss. One simple, thoughtless gesture of affection. Yet it spoke volumes. He was attracted to Eva. He couldn't deny it any longer. Okay, more than attracted. He'd always liked her. A lot. But over the past few weeks those feelings had exploded into a craving to see her again and again. And it was futile. He was leaving soon. It was time for him to pull away from Eva. To put some distance between them.

So, why had he invited her to ride with him to the investigation meeting later this afternoon? Ah, he didn't know why. It was crazy, but his thoughts deceived him. He couldn't seem to help himself. It was as though he didn't understand his own mind. More and more he found himself thinking about her when he should have been concentrating on work. He longed to be near her at every opportunity. He felt happy when she was around. As though the pain of the past wasn't important anymore. But that didn't mean he was going to get any closer to Eva than he already was. No matter how desirable she was. No matter how good she smelled or how pretty she looked when she was holding baby Cody. He couldn't let it impact him. And that was that.

He slid the electric screwdriver and one camera mount into the pocket of his jacket. He walked over to the ladder and climbed up fast. Eva stood at the bottom, holding it steady.

"Has Ben's condition changed at all?" he called over his shoulder.

"No, I'm afraid not. He just lies there as though he were sleeping." Her voice sounded sad and forlorn. And once again he wished there was something he could do.

At least he could put up the surveillance cameras. Above all else, he wanted Eva, Mamie and the baby to be safe.

"Don't give up hope. Many people come out of these comas and do just fine," he said.

"I won't. Ben is constantly in my prayers. Grady, too. I'm sure God has a plan in mind for both of them."

She sounded so certain. So convinced. But Tyler had his doubts. He wanted to encourage her, but he knew medically that Ben's condition would only deteriorate the longer he stayed in the coma. Maybe it was time for him to exercise a little faith and trust in the Lord.

"You really do believe in God's will, don't you?" he asked. He braced the mount against the rough wood siding and marked the spot with a pencil. Then he reached for the electric screwdriver.

"I do. Over the years, the Lord has been a constant source of strength for me. I have to trust in Him. I wish you would, too," she said.

The whirring zip of the screwdriver filled the air as he installed the mount. Eva's words spoke to his heart. He wanted to trust the Lord to heal his broken soul, but didn't quite know how to let go of his anger and hurt. At the same time, he wondered if maybe the first step was to give God a second chance.

"You could start by joining us at church on Sunday," she suggested.

He chuckled. "Okay. I can take a hint."

But he didn't say he would be there. That kind of commitment scared him too much. He figured the Lord didn't have time for him, so why should he bother with God?

"I think Aunt Mamie will feel better once these cameras are in place," Eva said in a conversational voice.

And so would Eva, if he read her right. And that bothered him intensely. He didn't want her to be afraid.

"Yeah, I wish I'd had some cameras put up out at my place before Applejack was stolen. If we had, we might have caught the thief," he said.

"The cameras might not be of much help," she said. "I heard that Carson Thorn had put some up at his place, but the thief got around them anyway."

He nodded, aiming the camera down toward the area below. "This surveillance system isn't foolproof. Just an added precaution. But so many of the local ranchers are putting them up on their property that we're bound to catch something. Even a tiny glimpse of the thief might lead to his identity."

"Does it seem like the losses of some of the ranchers are the gains of the struggling ranchers?" Eva asked.

"Yes, it does." He gripped the ladder on both sides and stepped down.

"Do you think there's a connection between the two?"

He stood on the ground, accepting the next camera she placed in his hands. "I don't know, but I intend to speak with Sheriff Benson about it at our investigation meeting later this afternoon."

"Good. I think it's an important question we should ask."

"I agree. You're a smart lady, Eva Brooks."

She flashed a smile so bright that it made his chest ache. Sunlight gleamed against her long, red hair. Her soft brown eyes sparkled. A hum of happiness pumped through his veins. His breath caught in his throat. She was absolutely stunning. He tried to remind himself that she was just a friend. But convincing himself of that fact was getting harder by the minute.

Chapter Eleven

"I can't believe the camera system is finally finished and working," Eva said.

Sitting in the passenger's seat of Tyler's truck, she glanced over at him and smiled. A sense of relief blanketed her. The thefts had made her uneasy, but the cameras made her feel better.

"I'm glad I could help out." Tyler smiled and gripped the steering wheel with both hands. As he pulled onto the dirt road leading out of Stillwater Ranch, he gazed out the windshield.

"I hope we didn't take you away from something important today," Eva said.

"Nothing that couldn't wait."

Making conversation was easy right now. Eva was so pleased by the work they'd accomplished. Having the surveillance cameras set up distracted her from her other troubles. At least for a while.

"It was easier installing your system, I think, because I had already learned a few things by installing the cameras out at my place," Tyler said.

He sounded kind and genuine. Not at all irritated that he'd spent the majority of his day hooking up their cameras. As busy as he was, he'd taken the time without complaint and Eva was touched by his sacrifice.

As they transferred onto the paved road, he glanced in his rearview mirror. Eva gazed at his handsome profile, finally forcing herself to look away. Baby Cody was between them in his car seat, completely content. He chortled and looked up at them, his little forehead crinkled beneath his blue knit cap. Eva rested her arm along the edge of his seat and smiled down at him.

"I can't believe the change in him. He's really grown," Tyler remarked with a quick glance.

Eva chuckled. "A few weeks has made a big difference. I'm sure glad he got over his colic."

Tyler nodded. "But I think it has something to do with you, too. You have an easy manner about you that probably reassures the baby. I hope you won't give up on having a family of your own one day."

Eva frowned, not liking where this conversation was headed. "To have a family, I'd have to get married first. And right now, I don't think that will ever be possible. At least, not for me."

He looked over at her, his eyes crinkled in a frown. "Why not?"

She shrugged, wishing she'd never told him about her problem. "Because I can never be certain my husband won't resent me for not being able to give him children."

"He wouldn't if he really loves you. Your husband

shouldn't care that you can't have kids. He should be more concerned about you and your needs and desires."

She snorted. "That's how it might start out, but over time he'd come to hate me. And I'd rather not take that chance. I'm resigned to remaining single for the rest of my life."

His eyebrows knit together in a frown. "That's a daunting prospect. Besides, there are men out there who don't want children. You could marry one of them."

That made her freeze and she didn't speak for several moments. His comment made her face her own values. Her own beliefs. "I guess I love kids so much that it never occurred to me that I could marry someone who didn't want them. But somehow, I don't think that would make me happy. I think I'd like my husband to want children, too."

"That's understandable. You can still have a family even if you can't give birth. Adoption is one answer. There's also surrogacy."

She shook her head emphatically. "No, surrogacy isn't for me. I've heard of some success stories, but I've heard of horror stories, too. The surrogate sometimes changes her mind and wants to keep the baby, or she hounds the adoptive couple for money or wants to be included in the family life of the child. It all sounds rather upsetting to me. But I could easily accept a child through traditional adoption."

"Well, someone like you should be madly in love and happy with the man you marry," he said.

"I agree, but no. I don't think I'd dare try falling in love ever again. The last time hurt too much. Love is for people like you, Carson Thorn and Ruby Donovan."

Carson and Ruby were newly engaged to be married. Whenever Eva saw them together, they were the epitome of two lovebirds. Holding hands. Looking at each other with adoration. Ruby had even mentioned that she planned to have several children. Eva envied the love they shared. Their deep and abiding happiness together.

Tyler reached over and squeezed her hand. A simple gesture of kindness, but she moved her hand away.

He glanced over at her and frowned. "Marriage should be built on trust and respect, Eva. Nothing else will last. When Kayla broke up with me, I realized she didn't really love me. Not if she didn't want me to keep my promise to the league and return to Little Horn for one year. You have to trust your husband to do the right things, just as he has to trust you. It's a two-way street built on mutual respect."

Misgivings settled like a sack of rocks in her stomach. "Yeah, I tried that once already, and look how it turned out. A complete failure."

She couldn't prevent a bit of resentment from entering her voice. She sounded hurt and bitter, probably because she was. Yet that wasn't who she wanted to be. She wanted to be happy. To feel content with her life. To have confidence in herself. To love and trust just one special man who felt the same way about her. But all of that seemed so elusive right now. And it did her no good to entertain such possibilities.

"Craig wasn't the right man for you," Tyler said.

"You've got that right." And she would have laughed if it hadn't been so sad.

"He didn't deserve someone as wonderful as you."

Eva didn't respond to that, but she turned away and wiped her cheek. She hated to let Tyler see her cry. She swallowed, feeling as though she had a brick stuck in her throat.

"I'm sorry he hurt you," he said.

"Yeah, me too. Can we change the subject now?" she asked.

He showed a tender smile, as though he were trying to take away her pain. "Of course. I'm sorry I ever brought it up."

She was, too. Because it was a reminder of what she could never have. At least Craig had broken up with her before the wedding. If they'd got married first, she would have been utterly crushed. Maybe she should be grateful for that small favor. But now that Tyler knew her deep, dark secret, she felt vulnerable. As though she was somehow unworthy of anyone's love.

They arrived in town, and Tyler drove them down Main Street. As he pulled into a vacant spot in the league's parking lot, Eva noticed the sheriff's squad car and a variety of other vehicles parked nearby. She glanced at her watch and realized they were five minutes late.

"Looks like we're the last to arrive," Tyler said as he killed the engine.

She caught no resentment in his tone, but couldn't help feeling a bit embarrassed. Their departure from the ranch had been delayed when she'd had to change

Cody's diaper. But more than that, she'd been stunned when Tyler had helped her with the chore. He'd folded and carried the poopy diaper outside to the garbage can while Eva had dressed the baby in clean clothes. Even without being married, she knew it was a rare man who would jump in and help change a baby's dirty diaper.

"I'm sorry about that," she said.

He gave a careless shrug of his wide shoulders. "Babies require attention. It was no problem. The meeting will proceed with or without us. It'll be fine."

His reassurance made her feel a tad better. He opened his door and climbed out. While Tyler hurried around to help her get the baby out, Eva unclicked the car seat. She climbed out of the truck and reached back in to lift out Cody's carrier.

"I've got it." Tyler took the weight with his own hands and carried the baby into the building. Eva followed with the diaper bag.

Ingrid Edwards, the league's secretary, sat at the front reception desk. The moment Tyler walked inside, the woman popped out of her seat, a wide smile on her face.

"Well, hello, Dr. Grainger," she called.

Tyler was occupied with Cody and barely spared her a glance. "Hi, Ingrid."

The woman bent over the baby, her spectacles sliding down her nose. She pushed them up and reached out to caress Cody's little hand. The cloying scent of Ingrid's heavy perfume filled the air and Eva held her breath.

"Oh, what a sweetheart," Ingrid chirped. "I love

children. Did you know that? Someday I'm gonna have a dozen babies. How about you? Would you like lots of children, Dr. Grainger?"

Eva bit her tongue, trying not to laugh. Everyone in town knew that Ingrid was on the prowl for a husband. She'd made some vow to herself that she'd be married by the time she turned twenty-six. And it appeared that any eligible bachelor was fair game, including Tyler. But the woman was so obvious about it that it made everyone a bit uncomfortable.

Tyler didn't seem to notice. He glanced at the hallway leading to the boardroom. "Uh, yeah. Is everyone in the meeting already?"

"Yes. You can go on in. I brought snacks for all of you to munch on." Ingrid tucked a limp strand of hair back behind her ear, her voice filled with eagerness. "Do you need me to watch the baby for you?"

"Thank you, but that won't be necessary," Eva said, trying to be as pleasant as possible.

She followed Tyler down the hallway, feeling a bit territorial. And she wondered why that was. Tyler wasn't her boyfriend. She had no right to feel jealous. But she did.

Tyler opened the hardwood door and stepped aside for Eva to precede him into the boardroom. The heavy aroma of coffee filled the air.

"Oh, good. Tyler and Eva are here." Sheriff Benson stood at the front of the room, as though she'd been waiting for them.

Tom and Amanda sat nearby. They each greeted them with a wave. A variety of cookies, peanut brittle and fruitcake sat on the table for them to eat.

"Sorry we're late, everyone. The baby delayed us a few minutes," Eva said.

"No problem. We're just glad you're here," the sheriff said.

Eva sat near the door, in case Cody got fussy and she needed to take him out. Tyler sat beside her. Without asking, he reached into the carrier, unclicked the straps and picked up the baby. Like always, he crossed an ankle over his knee and set Cody on his thigh, lightly bouncing the baby as he listened to the discussion.

Amanda tossed a knowing smile in Eva's direction. Eva groaned inwardly. No doubt Amanda thought that she and Tyler were an item. But Eva thought she'd only make things worse if she said something about it.

The sheriff pointed at a dry-erase board where she'd listed two columns of names. Thefts and gifts. Eva recognized the names as those ranchers who'd received gifts from the anonymous benefactor and those who had been the victims of theft. Tyler's name was included. More and more it appeared that they'd never recover his sister's mare.

"Okay, let's recap our discussion," the sheriff said. "I've researched Tyler's idea that maybe the stolen cattle and equipment were being re-homed to the struggling ranchers in the area."

"Like a Robin Hood stealing from the rich to give to the poor?" Amanda Jones said.

The sheriff nodded. "Exactly like Robin Hood."

"Do you think it's Amelia Klondike?" Tom Horton asked. "She started the Here to Help group at church and is always out helping others. Plus, she's wealthy. She doesn't need to steal in order to help others."

The sheriff shook her head. "No, I've spoken to Amelia at length and she vehemently denies being the benefactor. Plus, I have no proof that she's the thief. Nor do I believe she'd do such a thing. There's no evidence linking her to the crimes. And I know the stolen property isn't being re-homed. People are receiving gifts of brand-new items, not old stolen property."

"But what if the thief is selling the goods and using the money to buy new stuff to distribute to the struggling ranchers?" Tyler said.

Sheriff Benson nodded. "I checked into that, too. There's no way to track the purchases because we have no idea where the goods came from in the first place, but I doubt the thief would get much money for some of the stolen equipment. It's used, so they couldn't get full value for the items. They'd need more money."

"Someone like Amelia has lots of money available," Tom said.

"Yes, but again, I have no reason to believe that she's the thief or the benefactor," the sheriff said.

Tyler listened to the conversation with rapt attention. If Amelia Klondike wasn't the benefactor, then who was? It didn't make sense. There had to be a connection somewhere.

"Do you think the thefts and gifts are linked in some way?" he asked.

The sheriff nodded. "I do. I can't tie them together,

but my gut instinct tells me they're related. I just don't know how. But I do believe this is definitely a Robin Hood type of situation. Taking from the rich and giving to the poor."

As he listened, Tyler lifted the baby up to his shoulder. Cody squirmed and promptly spit up on Tyler's shirt. Without missing a beat, Eva quickly grabbed a burp cloth out of the diaper bag and blotted the white smudge. Tyler didn't mind. As a pediatrician, it wasn't the first time he'd been spit up on. He took it as a common hazard of being around kids. No big deal. But Eva's cheeks flamed red with embarrassment.

"It's okay." He gave her a smile of reassurance and she relaxed again.

"I've made some inquiries to see if we can trace where the gifts of hay and horses might have come from. I should have more information tomorrow morning," the sheriff said.

"In the meantime, is there anything we can do to help you out?" Tyler asked.

"Yeah, the Martelli Ranch lost some cattle and equipment last night. They called to report the theft to me just before this meeting. As soon as we're finished here, I'm on my way over to take a look at the crime scene."

"I can help you as soon as I drop Eva off at Stillwater Ranch," Tyler said. He faced Eva to get her reaction. "Does that sound okay to you?"

It was late enough in the afternoon that he figured Eva wouldn't want to accompany him with the baby in tow. It was too cold outside. But he waited for her opinion.

"Yes, thank you. I'd appreciate that."

They discussed a few more issues, and then the meeting broke up. Tyler escorted Eva outside. She flipped a light blanket over the baby's carrier, to protect Cody's tiny lungs from the chilly breeze. It was dark enough that the streetlights had come on, gleaming in the dusky night.

"I'm sorry you have to take Cody and me home before you go over to the Martelli place," Eva said.

"It's no bother. You're more important to me right now," he said.

And he meant it. He stared into her clouded eyes and realized he cared about this woman. Probably too much.

"I wish I could go with you to the Martellis', to help with the investigation," she said. "It'll be dark and you'll need someone to help hold the lights so you can lay out the crime scene."

He wished she could go with him, too. But his reasons were purely selfish. He didn't want to be parted from her even for a minute.

"It's okay. Tom will be there and you've got this little guy to care for." He lifted Cody's carrier into the truck and secured it with the seat belt.

Turning, he helped Eva climb up and then closed her door. Her eyes were wide and haunted by painful regrets. Things that were out of her control. And he hated that her former fiancé had made her feel as though she wasn't worthy of love.

Walking around to the driver's seat, Tyler tried to collect his thoughts. He felt confused. He'd thought he had everything planned out so well. But now he wondered if he should scrap his plans in Austin and do something else. His career would suffer for it. And he'd worked so hard. He was just feeling compassionate for Eva's plight. Worrying about her like he'd done when they'd been kids. It wasn't anything more. It couldn't be. She didn't want to get married and neither did he. It was that simple.

On the drive to Stillwater Ranch they didn't speak a lot. Both of them seemed lost in their own thoughts.

"Are you okay?" he asked finally.

"I'm just dandy."

That answer again. He was getting the impression that she was trying to convince herself. A myriad of thoughts came to his mind. Words of encouragement. Statements about love, marriage and children. He'd get himself into a whole heap of trouble if he said those things out loud. Not only because Eva wouldn't like it, but also because he was trying very hard not to fall in love with this woman who'd written off ever marrying.

"Do you really think we've got a Robin Hood–type thief in the area?" Eva asked.

He nodded. "Yes, I do. We just haven't found the connection yet, but we will."

At Stillwater Ranch, he escorted Eva and the baby into the house. A bright moon gleamed in the sky. The fertile fields rolled out around them, the barren trees reaching their branches upward.

Miss Mamie called to them from the spacious living room. "Hello, you two. You'll stay for supper, won't you, Dr. Grainger?"

Tyler waved as they entered. "Sorry, but I can't. I've got another appointment."

He set the baby carrier on the floor, and Miss Mamie lifted Cody out and pulled the knit cap off his head.

Eva faced Tyler. "Thanks again for all your help today."

"You're welcome." He gazed into her eyes, wishing more than anything that he could stay. But no. He had to get out of here. Before he said something they both might regret.

Chapter Twelve

On Sunday morning, Eva settled onto a pew with Aunt Mamie and the baby. Soft organ music filtered through the air, a gentle hymn that set a reverent tone in the chapel. Cody lay in his carrier, gazing up at the wooden beams and ornate lights overhead. Eva reached out and scooped the baby into her arms. Glancing up, she tensed as Tyler walked into the room with his mother. Holding her son's arm, Veola beamed a happy smile. Several people gathered around to welcome them, including Carson Thorn, Ruby Donovan and John Mathers.

Eva ducked her head and peered at Tyler out of the corner of her eye. Dressed in a dark suit with a white shirt and purple paisley tie, he smiled and looked about the room with interest. His thick, blond hair was parted on the side, his face freshly shaved. He looked handsome, as if he'd just walked off the cover of *GQ* magazine. Ingrid Edwards rushed over to him, chatting and laughing like a silly girl.

Eva looked away, focused on Cody. She cuddled

the baby close, breathing in his warm, sweet skin. Remembering her previous conversations with Tyler, she wondered what had got him to come to church today. She thought he wanted nothing to do with God. Since he planned to leave town in a matter of days, she couldn't help thinking this was a rare occasion. But a good one.

"Mind if we sit with you?"

Eva snapped her head around. Tyler stood beside her, his mother in tow.

"Hello! Of course. Good morning." She smiled at Veola.

"Good morning, Eva." The woman reached across Tyler and caressed Cody's arm. "Can I hold the baby?"

Eva nodded and handed Cody over. As she did so, she noticed several people looking her way. A low murmur permeated the reverent atmosphere. No doubt everyone was surprised to see Tyler here. But the fact that he'd chosen to sit next to Eva gave them extra fodder for discussion.

Some waved. Others bent their heads together to discuss this turn of events.

"Oh, no," she groaned.

"What's the matter?" he said.

"You and I are now officially the hot topic of the day," she whispered.

He looked around, then gave a careless shrug. "So let them talk."

"No, it's not good. You're about to leave town, and everyone will think I've been jilted again." Thinking about it, her cheeks heated up like a flamethrower.

She'd been so embarrassed when Craig had dumped her. The pain and humiliation almost had been more than she could bear. Feeling as though no one wanted her. As if she was a pariah. She didn't want to give the gossips something else to talk about, yet she liked being near Tyler.

His shoulders stiffened and he didn't look as calm and collected anymore. "Oh, I'm sorry, Eva. I didn't think about that. I can sit somewhere else."

He started to rise, but she tugged on his arm. "No, please stay. We're friends, and I'm glad to see you at church."

He gave her a sheepish grin. "Yeah, I figured it was about time."

It occurred to Eva that Tyler didn't want to cause her any problems. That he really cared about her feelings. But that wouldn't stop the gossips from having their say. And then Eva realized she was thinking too much about what other people might say and not enough about Tyler's well-being. It was time she lived her life without fear. Without being motivated by what other people thought of her.

"What made you decide to come?" she asked.

"You did. You have such a strong faith. And I envy that. So I decided to do something about it."

His words touched her heart.

"Well, it's good to see you here," she said.

He flushed red. "It's good to be here, too. I think."

She took a settling breath, letting herself relax. "This was a good choice."

"You don't think the ceiling will fall in on us, do you?" he asked with a lopsided grin.

She quirked one eyebrow. "Of course not. Why?"

"Because I walked into the Lord's house."

She gave a low laugh. "Actually, I think God is smiling today. I'm sure He's glad you're here, too."

Tyler settled one hand on his thigh, his fingers brushing against her leg. "You are?"

"Yes, very much so."

"Shh," Aunt Mamie hushed them. "The service is about to start. Don't make me separate you two kids."

Glancing up, Eva saw her aunt's eyes twinkle with mirth. Separating her and Tyler was obviously the last thing on Mamie's mind. She was delighted they were sitting together.

Eva went very quiet, bowing her head as the congregation prayed. She lifted her voice when they sang. Tyler's rich baritone sounded beside her. And she became conscious of him listening intently to a talk about loving your neighbor and leaving judgments up to the Lord. Just what Eva needed to hear.

Sitting so close to Tyler, she caught his spicy scent and breathed in deeply. Aunt Mamie squeezed her hand and Eva couldn't help smiling. She felt happy today. As though she really belonged here. With Tyler Grainger. An insane notion considering his imminent departure. But she decided to ignore that for now. He was here today, and maybe she'd played a part in bringing him back to the Lord. And then a thought struck her like a cannonball. Something that took her completely off guard.

She loved Tyler. Right there, in the middle of the church meeting, surrounded by members of her community, Eva realized she loved him. Loved his kindness, loved his nonjudgmental attitude, his easygoing manners, his loyalty, his support. She loved the way his chin hardened when he was concentrating and the way his eyes softened every time he looked at her. Tyler was a good man. Generous and giving. She loved everything about him. And the thought came upon her so suddenly that she actually jerked. Her pulse sped up into double time, her breath rushing out in a lung-squeezing sigh.

"Are you okay?" he whispered close to her ear.

She tingled as his breath teased a wispy curl beside her cheek. She tightened her hands in her lap, letting the truth settle over her like a damp blanket. What could she do now?

"Y-yes," she stuttered, her throat suddenly dry as sandpaper. Because it would hurt so much when he left town in another week. Tyler was her dearest friend. Someone she could talk to. A man she'd confided her deepest, darkest secrets to. But loving him would lead to nothing but more heartache.

Tyler wondered if he shouldn't have come here today. Maybe this was a mistake. Maybe he'd been gone so long that the Lord had forgotten all about him. Yet he wanted to be closer to God and realized attending the church services could help with that. To work out his own salvation.

Eva stared at the pulpit, listening intently to the speaker. She looked beautiful with her long, red hair pulled back and lying about her shoulders in soft curls. She wore a flower-print dress and a red matching jacket and sky-high heels. He gazed at her trim ankles, thinking there must be oodles of men lined up at her door.

The speaker read some scriptures about loving your neighbor as yourself. Tyler tried to focus. The message sank deep into his soul. He'd been serving this community for a year now and he realized he loved these people. No doubt about it.

Over the next thirty minutes he let the word of God permeate his hardened heart. With his mom sitting on one side of him and Eva on the other, he felt perfectly complete. As if he really belonged here.

Veola lifted Cody up to her shoulder. The baby bopped Tyler on the arm with his tiny fist. Tyler gazed into the baby's big brown eyes. Cody smiled and bopped him some more. Tyler couldn't resist and took the baby into his arms. Cody settled against the crook of his elbow, tugging at the collar of his white shirt, completely fascinated by the bright color of his tie.

Eva reached up and spread a burp cloth over Tyler's shoulder, obviously to protect his suit from any spit-up. Tyler liked the gesture and flashed Eva a warm smile of gratitude. She was always so considerate. So gentle and refined. The perfect woman. If only she wasn't harboring a broken heart. If only they'd met again under different circumstances. If only he wasn't returning to Austin in another week.

If only she hadn't sworn off marriage.

He mentally shook his head. It did no good to think about all the what-ifs. His life was filled with them. And right now he needed to focus on finishing his work here in Little Horn, boxing up his office and getting back to his business in Austin. He had people counting on him there. A comfortable condo. Membership at the golf club. A lucrative career waiting for him.

He bowed his head during the closing prayer, trying to focus on what was being said. Trying not to feel confused and sad.

"Dr. Grainger?"

He turned his head. Grace Bingham, the nurse from the hospital, stood in the middle of the aisle. She wore her green smock and white slacks, a name badge pinned to her lapel.

Organ music filled the air in a soft hymn, signaling it was time for everyone to move on to their Sunday-school classes. People stood and crowded the aisles, greeting one another, parents ushering their children off to class. Ingrid Edwards hovered nearby, probably hoping to speak with him again. But right now Tyler didn't have patience for her nonsense. The only woman he was interested in was Eva.

He stood and shifted Cody to his other shoulder. "Hi, Grace. What's up?"

"I'm sorry to interrupt," she said. "I tried to call your cell phone, but you're not picking up. I remembered this morning when you made your hospital rounds that you said you were going to church today. Since it's such a short walk, I came over to get you."

As if on cue, Eva stood and held out her arms, and Tyler handed Cody over to her. He reached into his pants pocket for his cell phone and quickly turned on the volume. "Yes, I turned off the sound just for a short time so I wouldn't disturb the meeting. Who's the doctor on call?"

"Dr. Copeland. But the patient is six years old, so he thought it might be better to call you in."

"Okay. What's the problem?"

After all, he wasn't on call. But he knew emergencies came up now and then.

She gave him a half smile and leaned closer to whisper the private information for his ears alone. "A patient has come into the hospital. Little Amy Callister. She's very ill. It's serious, Doctor. She can't breathe well. We don't know what's wrong. Can you come now?"

His heart fluttered. This was why he'd become a doctor. To help kids. To do his best to ensure they got better.

"Yes, of course." He glanced at his mother. "But how will you get home?"

"I can take her," Eva volunteered.

He looked down, his eyes meeting hers. His wonderful Eva. Maybe she couldn't cook, but she always seemed to be there when he needed her. Always seemed to know what was right.

"I'd appreciate it." He touched her hand in a show of appreciation.

She shifted Cody to her hip. "It's my pleasure."

Veola tugged on his arm. "Go on now, son. I'll be fine. Help that little girl."

Tyler slipped past her and followed Grace to the outer door. Carson Thorn tried to intercept him.

"Have you got a minute?"

"Not right now. I've got an emergency at the hospital. Can we talk later?" Tyler said.

"Sure. This can wait." Carson nodded his understanding and let him go.

As Tyler ran outside into the morning sunshine, the chilling breeze rushed past, bringing the scent of rain. He barely noticed as he hopped into his truck, turned on the engine and followed Grace. He'd wanted to talk to Eva before he left, but wouldn't get the chance now. And quite frankly, he wasn't sure what he should say to her. He enjoyed her companionship, but wished he could say something to give her hope. He thought of asking her to go to Austin with him, but doubted she'd accept. She was a small-town girl. A family girl. She deserved a husband and kids, but it didn't appear she'd ever get them. It appeared as though she'd live her life as a single woman. And that thought made him feel empty and cold inside.

All of that would have to wait for now. Refocusing on his work, he thought about the Hippocratic oath he'd taken a few years earlier. To help his patients. To do the best he could. And one thought pounded his brain. He had to get to the hospital fast. He had to help little Amy Callister.

Chapter Thirteen

Eva stepped into the hospital and headed straight for the intensive care unit. She carried a small teddy bear. A gift for Amy Callister. She'd left Cody home, planning to visit Ben first, then see how Amy was doing before she stopped at the grocery store on her way home. The whole town was talking about Amy. It seemed her condition was very serious, her parents beside themselves with worry.

As she walked the long, sterile hallway, Eva glanced about, wondering if Tyler was here. They hadn't spoken since he'd dashed out of the church house two days earlier and she wondered how he was doing.

"Hi, Eva. You here to visit Ben?" Grace Bingham greeted her at the nurses' station. Holding a clipboard in one hand, the woman smoothed the other one over her blue smock and showed a bright smile.

"Yes. Good morning. Has there been any change?" Eva indicated Ben's room. She'd asked this question a zillion times, but the answer was always the same. She hoped that one day she'd get a different answer.

"Nope, I'm afraid not." Grace shook her head, her eyes filled with sorrow.

"I was hoping he'd come out of it soon," Eva said.

"I know, but his vital signs are strong. Sometimes, these things take time. Don't give up hope."

"I won't. You can never give up on family." Eva nodded her thanks before stepping into Ben's room. Like always, he lay completely still, his handsome face turned toward the window. Sunlight streamed through the slatted blinds. His chin showed a light stubble and she figured the hospital staff hadn't shaved him yet that morning. His cheeks looked slightly hollowed. A sure sign he was losing weight. In fact, his condition broke Eva's heart. Ben had always been so strong and vital. So full of life.

Sitting beside him, she held his hand.

"Hi, sweetheart," she said to him, hoping he could hear her even if he couldn't respond. "How are you doing today? We're missing you out at the ranch."

She told him about the surveillance system Tyler had helped her install and plans for the annual Thanksgiving banquet over at the league building in a couple more days.

"Cody's about four months old now. He's getting good with his hands. And his neck is so strong. He can reach for toys, but of course everything goes right into his mouth." She chuckled, telling Ben all about the baby's progress.

Before she left she whispered a quick prayer. That God would help Ben recover. It'd be the best Thanksgiving ever if only Ben would come out of his coma and Grady would come home safely from Afghanistan.

She paused beside the front desk and glanced over at Grace.

"You haven't seen Tyler Grainger, by chance?" she asked.

"Yes, as a matter of fact, I have. He spends a lot of time with Amy Callister."

Hmm. Not surprising. Eva knew Tyler was a dedicated doctor. But she'd heard that he'd barely left Amy's side since she'd come into the hospital.

"Any idea what's wrong with her?" Eva asked.

Grace shook her head. "I'm afraid I can't discuss that, Eva. Patient confidentiality and all. I'm sorry."

"I understand. Thank you." Eva stepped away and headed down the hall.

She couldn't fault Grace. The nurse was only doing her job. But Eva was worried about Amy. In a small town this size, everyone knew everyone else. Amy was a sweet girl. Her father was an auto mechanic at the local garage, and her mom was always active in bake sales at the church.

Eva was worried about Tyler, too. He hadn't attended the investigation team meeting the day before. The sheriff had said he didn't dare leave Amy and that the little girl wasn't doing well. Knowing Tyler, he took that personally. If Amy didn't recover, Eva worried how it might impact Tyler.

She loved him. And she couldn't fight off the urge to know that he was okay. She paused outside little Amy's room and peeked inside. A white curtain hung from the ceiling, partially concealing the room.

Eva stepped just inside the doorway. Tyler wasn't there. Amy lay on the bed, her eyes closed, her face as pale as death. An oxygen mask covered the child's mouth and nose. Her rasping breath told Eva the girl wasn't breathing normally. A soft spot opened up in Eva's heart. She couldn't stand the thought that Amy might not survive. No matter how hard Eva tried not to care about other people's kids, she couldn't seem to help herself. She wanted Amy to run and laugh like all children should. To live a long, happy life.

The bathroom door creaked. Elaine Callister, Amy's mama, stepped out carrying a pitcher of water. Seeing Eva, the woman jerked in surprise.

"Oh, Eva. I didn't know you were here."

Eva stepped closer, wanting to comfort Elaine. She spoke in a whisper so she wouldn't disturb the sleeping child. "Hello, Elaine. I just wanted to stop by and see how Amy is doing."

She handed the teddy bear to Elaine. The woman stared at it with wide, bloodshot eyes.

"Oh, that's so kind of you." Elaine set the pitcher on the tray table beside the bed and her shoulders slumped. She squeezed the bear, hugging it close against her chest. When she spoke, her low voice sounded tired and scratchy. "She's not doing well. She's been running a high fever and having trouble breathing."

Eva's heart squeezed. "That's not good. Any idea what's wrong?"

"Yes, she has enterovirus. Dr. Grainger just gave us the test results early this morning. Apparently there's a small outbreak of the disease across the country. There's no telling when Amy will be off the ventilator. Dr. Grainger said her case is much worse than usual. She's just not getting any better."

Eva rested her hand on Elaine's arm in a gentle show of support. "I'm so sorry to hear that. Is there anything I can do?"

"Just pray for us. Please." Her voice held a hint of desperation.

Eva inclined her head. "Sure I will. And can I sit with Amy for some time while you go and get some rest?"

Elaine waved a hand. "Oh, no. I'm not going anywhere. Not until I know my baby is out of harm's way."

Eva couldn't blame her. If this were her child, she wouldn't leave, either. Not for a single minute. "I can certainly understand that. But try to get some rest."

Elaine nodded. "I will. Thanks for stopping by."

Eva stepped outside and came face-to-face with Tyler. He bumped into her side.

"Eva! I didn't know you were here."

"Hi, Tyler. Yes, I came by to see Amy…and you." She pulled the strap of her purse up over her shoulder.

"That's very kind." He sounded stilted, his gaze wandering to Amy's bed.

No doubt he had a lot on his mind and was distracted by his sick patient. His clothes were rumpled and he looked weary, the shadow of whiskers on his face. From what Eva could see, he hadn't slept much in the past couple of days, watching over Amy as if she were his own child.

"Elaine just told me about Amy's condition. I've heard of enterovirus on the national news. It can be a nasty disease."

He heaved a heavy sigh and spoke in a whisper.

"Yeah, Amy's case is pretty bad. Thankfully, this virus is self-limiting. Normally the patient gets better within a few days. But no matter what I do, Amy doesn't seem to be responding."

"I heard that she also has asthma. Do you think that's exacerbating the problem?"

He released a heavy breath and his shoulders slumped with the exhalation. "I'm sure it is."

He glanced toward the room, as if to assure himself that Elaine couldn't overhear his words. Eva heard the apprehension in his voice and saw the concern in his eyes. He was worried. Big-time. She wanted to comfort him. To see him smile again.

"Is there anything I can do?" Eva asked.

"No. All any of us can do is wait."

He wore a troubled frown.

"You're remembering Jenny, aren't you?" she asked.

He snapped his head around and gazed at her with wide eyes. "How did you know that?"

She touched his arm, wishing she dared give him a hug. "I know how much you miss your little sister, Tyler. I know it means a lot to you to save Amy's life. You're a very caring man."

She almost told him that was one of the reasons she loved him so much, but she clamped her mouth closed. Tyler had done all that he could for Amy. The situation was in God's hands now.

Tyler released a shallow breath and raked his fingers through his hair. He'd felt nervous and jittery, until Eva showed up. It was so good to see her. So good to know she was near. Somehow she made him feel as though everything would be okay. That there was hope for his sick patient.

"Is Amy's situation really all that bad?" Eva asked.

He nodded. "I'm afraid so. I...I've never lost a patient before, Eva."

His confession slipped out before he could stop it. He felt responsible for Amy. He was her doctor and her parents were looking to him for answers. But an icy fear gripped his heart. He took the little girl's condition personally. As though she were his own child. He couldn't lose her. Couldn't put her parents through that kind of grief. He'd always known that one day he might lose a patient, but now that he faced that possibility, he realized how little control he had over the situation.

"Have you prayed about it?" Eva asked.

He went very still. In all honesty, the thought of praying hadn't even entered his mind. He'd got so used to going it alone. Living his life without the Lord. Moving through life without asking for help from anyone. But maybe that should change. And fast. Before it was too late. Maybe he should try one more time. Because only God could make Amy well again.

"No, I haven't. Yet," he said.

He didn't like to tell Eva that. He thought about evading the question, but he couldn't lie. Not to her. She'd know the truth just by looking at his face. They seemed to have a unique bond he didn't quite understand. As though they could look deep inside and read each other's minds.

"Maybe it's time you talked to God about the problem," she said.

"Yes, maybe it is." Time to let the Lord back into

his life. Time to reprioritize and think about what he really wanted the most.

"You look tired and discouraged," she said.

"I'll be okay."

"Can't you get some rest?"

He hefted one shoulder. "My needs pale in comparison to Amy's needs. Nothing else matters right now."

"Don't give up, Tyler. The Lord can work miracles. They say it's always darkest before the dawn. Amy could still make a complete turnaround."

He wasn't so sure. It'd been a long time since he'd seen any miracles worked in his life. But Eva looked so earnest that he didn't want to hurt her feelings by saying that. Instead, he took strength from her faith. If Eva believed in God, then surely something good could come from that. He wanted to believe in the Lord. Wanted to know that someone really cared that much.

"Can I walk you out to your truck?" he asked, wanting to be with her a few minutes longer.

"Sure." She nodded and swiveled on her heels.

He escorted her outside into the sunshine. A chilling breeze swept over them and she shivered in her winter coat. He barely felt the cold. All he could think about was figuring out how to help Amy.

He opened Eva's truck door for her, eager to get her in out of the wind. "Thanks for stopping by. It was good to see you again."

She smiled at him and his gaze rested on her full lips. He was reminded of that time during the stakeout when he'd kissed her. He'd been so worried about her. So desperate to know that she was okay that he hadn't thought about what he was doing until it was too late. And now the memory haunted him. Whether he liked it or not, his heart was tied to Eva's. He loved her. It was that simple. And yet it wasn't.

"You must be excited to move back to Austin next week. Are you still planning to leave the day after Thanksgiving?" she asked as she tossed her purse onto the passenger seat.

He nodded, not feeling too excited about the prospect anymore. What had seemed so exciting only a few weeks earlier now seemed like doom and gloom. He had plans. Goals he'd worked hard to achieve all his life. And Eva had vowed never to marry.

So, where did that leave them? Nowhere. Not unless one or both of them was willing to change. Once he left Little Horn he wouldn't be able to see Eva regularly. Wouldn't be able to talk and laugh or share his deepest feelings with her. Yet he didn't know what else to do. He couldn't stay here and be near her. Not without making a fool out of himself and telling her how he really felt about her. She'd refuse his proposal and break his heart. Just like Kayla had done. And he didn't think he could go through that a second time.

"Yeah, it's what I'd planned ever since I was a kid," he said.

He remembered the hours he'd spent pondering his childhood dreams. But now those plans didn't hold the same kind of appeal. He loved his profession, but he sensed it wouldn't be as fulfilling without Eva by his side.

"What were your dreams as a child?" he asked.

She swallowed. "You already know."

"You…you wouldn't possibly consider moving to Austin, would you? To be with me?"

There. He'd said the words out loud. He'd exposed his heart, just to get a feel for how she might feel toward him. Trying to determine if she might make room for him in her life on a permanent basis.

She hesitated, then shook her head. "No, I'm afraid not. Little Horn is my home. It's where I'll always stay."

"You…you wouldn't reconsider marriage, would you?"

She tilted her head. "Is this a proposal?"

He gazed into her eyes. "And what if it were?"

She shook her head. "No, I'm afraid not."

"But what if I stayed here?"

Her brows arched. "You mean in Little Horn?"

"Yes."

She released a soft sigh, her gaze sliding away. "No. I'll never marry, Tyler. You already know my reasons why."

His heart hit the ground. Even if he was willing to stay here in Little Horn, she still wouldn't marry him.

"But I love you, Eva." Okay, his jugular was exposed. He'd laid it all out on the table. In fact, he'd do anything if only she'd say yes.

"Don't say that. Please. It'll only make things more difficult." She flashed a sad smile and got into the truck. He waited while she buckled her seat belt, inserted the key into the ignition and started the engine.

"You take care. We'll always be friends. I'll see you around sometime," she said.

"Yeah, see you around." He could barely speak around the spiky lump in his throat.

Friends. But that wasn't enough for him now. Not anymore.

He closed the door and stepped onto the sidewalk so she could back out. And as she pulled away, the thought occurred to him that, if he wanted Eva, if he really loved her, he'd have to convince her that she should marry him, kids or no kids. And right now he didn't know how to do that.

Hunching his shoulders against the cold, he slid his hands into his pockets and stood there watching her drive away. As she turned the corner, a jolt of pain hit him squarely in the chest. He was willing to give up his practice in Austin. Willing to adopt as many sweet children as Eva could handle. But how could he convince Eva to trust him? How could he break through the wall she'd built around herself? To prove that he loved her beyond her ability to give him children? No matter what he said, she wouldn't believe him. So what could he do?

Heaving a deep sigh, he gazed at the hospital, standing like a tall sentry against the hazy sky. Right now he couldn't think about these things. His thoughts were filled with misgivings. He had a very sick patient waiting inside. Amy Callister had to be his first priority right now. His relationship with Eva would have to wait.

He tried to tell himself he was doing what he wanted. Moving back to Austin. Resuming his old, cold life there. The lights, the action, the career he'd chosen for himself. But it no longer held the same attraction for him. Not without Eva. He just didn't know how to convince her they should be together. That loving him was worth a second chance. But he had to find a way. And soon.

Chapter Fourteen

Thanksgiving Day brought with it a flurry of snow that melted the moment it hit the pavement. In the wee hours of the morning, Eva got up and fed Cody, then rocked him as she sat beside her bedroom window and gazed out at the dreary sky. As the sun eased the power of darkness, leaden clouds filled the sky with gray. It mirrored the feelings in Eva's heart.

Tyler was leaving for Austin tomorrow. Up until now, she'd accepted that fact. She'd known of his plans for some time. But now she didn't want him to go. Of course, she couldn't tell him that. Never in a zillion years would she say or do anything to hold him back from meeting his dreams. He deserved to be happy. To have a lucrative career in Austin and oodles of children. And she would never say or do anything to ruin that for him.

Instead, she thought of all the things she was grateful for. Her home, family, good food to eat, medical care available at the drop of a hat. Little things she often took for granted.

As she padded barefoot to the kitchen, she caught the delicious aroma of cinnamon and allspice. Pumpkin pies Martha Rose had baked in the ovens last night. Eva thought about going back to bed and catching a couple more hours of sleep before Cody woke up again, but her thoughts swirled around inside her head, keeping her too preoccupied. She thought about how Tyler had held her in his strong arms, his warmth against her, the taste of his kiss on her lips.

Stop that. She mentally shook her head. She had to quit torturing herself like this. Had to let Tyler go.

Instead, she got ready for the day. She and Aunt Mamie would be leaving soon to drive into town and help set up the Thanksgiving buffet at the league's banquet hall. Aunt Mamie was eager to visit with her friends. With more than a hundred people expected for dinner, there was lots of work to do.

The morning seemed to whiz by in a blur. And before she knew it, Eva was standing inside the league building helping fold out chairs and tables.

"We're going to use these to cover each of the tables." Amelia Klondike held up a stack of inexpensive plastic white tablecloths.

"That's smart. They'll look nice and be easy for cleanup," Nelda Markham said.

Eva helped spread the cloths, then sprinkled fake autumn-colored leaves in the center of each table. Nelda and Olivia Barlow followed with miniature pumpkins and little gourds for decorations.

"Have you heard how Amy Callister is doing?" Nelda asked as they worked.

Eva jerked her head up, startled by the woman's

question, which was aimed at her. "Only that she's one sick little girl."

"I just thought since you've been spending so much time with Dr. Grainger that you might know something about her condition." Nelda's gray eyes twinkled with insinuation.

Eva shook her head. "Tyler and I are just good friends. But regarding Amy, I think everyone is just waiting and hoping for the best."

Nelda brushed a wrinkle out of a tablecloth. "Oh, I must have heard wrong, then."

Eva exhaled slowly. Hopefully the gossip would die down as soon as Tyler left town.

"I'm worried for Amy and her family," Olivia said. "This can't be easy on Elaine and David, watching their little girl lying so close to death."

Eva didn't respond, but she couldn't hold back a shiver of fear. She could only imagine how difficult it must be for Amy's parents and also for Tyler, not knowing what was going to happen. Eva wondered how parents could ever prepare themselves to face the worst. If they lost the child, she feared Tyler would feel responsible.

Lost in her thoughts, Eva went about her business, laying out paper napkins with a plump turkey and pumpkins stamped on the front. Then she helped Aunt Mamie bring in the pies and salads from their car. And soon the hall was filled with league members and their families. Over a hundred people congregated to share this special meal. Everyone laughed and joked. Even Veola Grainger showed up...without Tyler. Eva greeted the woman, going through the routine, but inside she felt a quiet sadness without Tyler's presence. She missed him, but realized she'd better get used to it.

Several plump, golden turkeys sat in the middle of the serving table. Two men were carving them up. Heaping bowls of mashed potatoes, gravy and stuffing showed the bounty of their feast. The aromas were tantalizing.

"Ahem. Welcome, everyone. Can I get you to quiet down for just a few minutes?" Carson Thorn stood at the front of the room, speaking into a microphone to get everyone's attention.

A hush fell over the group as they all turned to face him.

"The league wants to welcome you all to our annual Thanksgiving buffet. It's the season for gratitude, and the league thanks each one of you for your support. I've asked Jake Melton to offer a blessing on the food. I know many of us are worried about Amy Callister, too. So, I ask that you keep her in your thoughts and prayers, as well."

People nodded their heads as Carson stepped back and offered the mic to Jake. A former president of the league, the tall, rugged man whisked the black Stetson off his head before closing his eyes and lowering his chin.

In unison everyone bowed their heads as Jake offered a prayer in his deep voice. A prayer of gratitude for God and country. For the bounty in each of their lives. For family and friends. And for Amy's full recovery.

The ending of the prayer was the signal to eat.

The noise increased as everyone made a beeline for the buffet tables. Eva eyed the long line and then glanced at Cody.

"Aunt Mamie, would you like to wait here with the baby while I go get each of us a plate of food?"

"Yes, dear. That's just what I was thinking, too. Thank you." Holding the baby up, Aunt Mamie turned him so he could get a view of all the comings and goings in the room.

Cody's forehead crinkled, his big eyes wide and intelligent as he looked about with interest. More and more, he was looking just like his daddy. Except it was difficult to know if his father was Ben or Grady, since the men were identical twins.

Eva scooted her chair back and made her way over to the buffet line. She was standing there when Tyler walked in. Standing close by, she froze, hardly able to take her eyes off him. He wore his winter jacket over his white doctor's coat. Carson greeted him.

"Howdy, partner. I didn't think we'd get to see you today." Carson thrust out his hand in greeting.

Tyler shook the man's hand. "Hi there. Since the hospital is so close by, I just stopped by for a quick bite of food and to check on my mom. I hope that's okay. I can't stay long."

Tyler didn't smile as he ran a hand through his hair. He looked unshaven and haggard. As if he hadn't slept in days.

Eva stood at the back of the line. Tyler met her gaze, smiled and inclined his head. Her heart pounded and her knees went wobbly. But she hung back. Something had changed between them since they'd last met. Something she didn't understand. As though the barriers around their hearts had grown even thicker and taller. She thought about his invitation that she relocate to Austin. But she couldn't encourage him. He was the marrying kind. A family man. And maybe not right now, but eventually, he'd come to resent her because she couldn't have kids.

She didn't know how to scale the mountain of doubt standing between them. And wishing things could be different wouldn't change that. She figured it'd be best to leave Tyler alone right now. After all, he had other important matters on his mind.

"Let's get you through the line fast," Carson said. "Anything we can do to accommodate you."

Carson led Tyler to the front of the line. Most people didn't mind, but Byron McKay harrumphed with indignation. He stood in the line with his wife and teenage sons. Gareth and Winston each showed a sullen frown.

"Why is he getting preferential treatment?" Gareth grumbled.

"I don't know," Byron growled. "He should have stayed and eaten in the hospital cafeteria."

Standing behind the serving table, Amelia objected. "No way. It's Thanksgiving. Dr. Grainger needs a home-cooked meal before he has to rush back to the hospital to take care of Amy and his other patients."

Wearing a bright red-and-white-checkered apron, Amelia waved a spoon and beckoned to Tyler. He flashed a half smile of embarrassment as he stood before her. Amelia proceeded to spoon a giant portion of mashed potatoes and gravy onto his plate.

"It'd make the holiday even better if Sheriff Benson and the league's Rustling Investigation Team were doing a better job." Byron spoke conversationally, but loud enough for everyone standing in line to hear him well.

"What's that supposed to mean?" Tom Horton blurted from where he sat nearby. He held his hand in midair, the bite of cranberry salad on his spoon forgotten.

Byron met the man's angry glare. "Just what I said. You haven't found the rustlers yet. We should take a vote and fire the current investigation team before bringing in better detectives."

Tom bristled. Eva objected to Byron's words. The team had been working hard and doing everything possible to figure out who was behind the thefts.

"I already told you at our last league meeting. We're not electing different investigators. Now let it drop," Carson said.

Byron's jaw hardened. "If we get enough votes to impeach the current team, you'd have to hold another election."

"And who would you put on the team instead? Your own cronies and friends?" Amanda Jones demanded.

"Well, at least they'd do a better job," Byron blustered.

"Stop it," Tyler said. He spoke so soft and firm that everyone went suddenly very quiet.

They all looked at him, waiting. His hazel-green eyes flashed with fire. He looked absolutely furious.

"Are you listening to yourselves?" Tyler continued. "You're surrounded by food and all you can do is bicker. It's Thanksgiving Day. Sheriff Benson and the investigation team are doing the best that we can. And today isn't about pointing fingers. It's about gratitude. It's about being thankful for all the blessings in your life. Maybe you ought to think about that for once."

Without another word, he turned and went to sit beside his mother and Ruby Donovan. Everyone stared after him. Although Eva hadn't participated in the argument, even she felt shamed. She'd been feeling sorry for herself lately. And she realized that grateful people tended to be happier people. Maybe it'd do Byron McKay some good to appreciate others for once.

Watching Tyler as he bent over his plate, Eva wished he would have sat with her and Aunt Mamie to eat his meal. But his mom needed him, too. He seemed distracted and Eva knew he was eager to return to the hospital.

The line continued to move and Eva stood quietly awaiting her turn. Gareth McKay was chatting with seventeen-year-old Maddy Coles, a foster child who was involved with one of the league's work programs for youth. Gareth laughed at something Maddy said, then noticed his father's disapproving glare and quickly moved away.

Eva mentally shook her head. Byron McKay was a snob. He never had anything good to say about someone else. Always demanding. Always judgmental and negative. With all his wealth, she couldn't understand why he couldn't be nice at least part of the time.

Back at her table Eva set a plate of delicious food in front of her aunt. "Here you go."

"Oh, candied yams. My favorite," Aunt Mamie exclaimed.

They ate and visited with the other people around them. Eva did her best not to look over at Tyler. Although he sat nearby, she felt as though he were miles away. And the void between them filled up with nothing but crushed hopes.

The moment he'd walked into the room, Tyler had homed in on Eva. She'd stood at the back of the buffet line wearing a pair of black dress pants, low heels and a red sweater. Comfy, festive and elegant. Her face looked pale and angry as she'd listened to Byron McKay's diatribe over firing the investigation team.

Tyler wanted to say something to Eva. To laugh and talk like they used to do. They'd felt so comfortable together. But not tonight. Not anymore. His departure in the morning seemed to stand between them like a large, dangerous giant. Still, he couldn't leave without saying goodbye.

On his way over to the dessert table, he paused beside Miss Mamie and inclined his head. "Good evening, ladies."

"Hello, Dr. Grainger. Why didn't you and Veola join us for dinner?" Aunt Mamie scolded with a bright smile.

"Oh, I had some business to discuss with Carson. Are you enjoying your holiday?" His words were for

Mamie, but his gaze rested on Eva. In fact, he couldn't take his eyes off her as she balanced Cody in her left arm while eating with her right.

"Of course."

"I'm sorry about the outburst earlier," he said.

Mamie waved a hand in the air. "It wasn't your fault, son. That Byron McKay was never a nice man. Even as a kid, he was always causing trouble. His pappy spoiled him rotten, if you ask me. I was glad to see you stand up to him. Served him right."

Tyler chuckled. "I know, but I still don't like it."

"Are you all packed and ready to leave tomorrow?" Eva asked.

He caught an edge of reluctance in her voice. Or maybe he imagined it.

He heaved a heavy sigh. "Almost. I've been so busy over at the hospital that I haven't had time to finish boxing up my office. I'll have to get it all done in the morning."

"How is little Amy doing?" Miss Mamie asked.

He just shook his head, his heart feeling heavier than ever before. "Still the same. I'd feel better about leaving town if she was on the mend. I may have to delay my trip a day or two. I'll see how she's doing in the morning. I won't go until we know something one way or the other."

He just hoped the girl recovered. In fact, faced with the possibility of losing his first patient, Tyler had finally prayed for the first time in a very long time. So far he didn't think God was listening, but he kept trying to have faith. To trust in the Lord's will.

"Eva, I was wondering if I might—"

His cell phone rang, a loud, shrill buzz. He'd set the volume on high so he'd be sure to hear it above the noise in the room.

He reached into his pocket for the phone and glanced at caller ID. "It's the hospital. Excuse me, please."

Eva was looking at him, waiting expectantly, her brown eyes wide and alert.

He poked the answer button on his cell phone. "Hello?"

"Dr. Grainger? This is Grace Bingham from the hospital."

Something cold gripped him. His heart froze in his chest. He'd left instructions that the nurse was to call him if there was any change in Amy Callister's condition. And he expected the worst.

"Yes, what is it?"

"Can you return to the hospital now?" Grace said.

Tyler's heart plummeted. His hands shook like leaves in the wind. "Is Amy…?"

"It's amazing, but she's finally breathing on her own, Doctor. And her fever's broken, too. She's opened her eyes and asked for something to eat."

Tyler's shoulders slumped in relief. Finally. Finally some good news. Amy was hungry. She was awake and strong enough to ask for food.

"Yes, I'll come immediately," he said and hung up.

"What is it? What's happened?" Eva asked.

He smiled, wanting to share this good news with her. Wanting to pull her into his arms and kiss her lips and hold her close against his heart. It was Thanksgiving Day and he had so much to be grateful for.

"I've got good news. Amy's breathing on her own. She's hungry and wants something to eat."

"Well, how wonderful. Hunger is always a good sign," Miss Mamie said.

Tyler's smiled widened. He just couldn't help himself. He felt so relieved. So happy. If only Eva would budge on her vow never to marry...

"Yes, it's great news," he said. "She's on a non-invasive ventilator. I'm going over to the hospital now to take her off it. And then we'll see about giving her a light meal."

Eva's eyes shimmered with joy and she hugged Cody tight against her chest. "Oh, Tyler. I'm so happy with this news. What a great Thanksgiving Day."

"Yes, it's wonderful," someone nearby agreed.

Looking around, Tyler realized several people had overheard the news. He hadn't meant to advertise it. But he was so excited that the words had just slipped out.

"Hey, did you hear that?" Tom Horton told Amelia Klondike. "The doc's done it. Amy Callister's gonna be okay."

Tyler stared at the people around him. He hadn't expected this outcome. The worry everyone had been feeling over Amy's condition. Their concern and delight now that she was out of danger. But he couldn't deal with it just now. He had to go.

He turned, seeking Eva out with his gaze. She sat holding the baby, her smile glowing like the flame from a candle. And he realized his first thought was of her. He wanted to share everything with her. His love, his life. Nothing seemed real until he'd told it to her.

He looked at her. She was smiling brightly. And he saw the approval in her eyes. The joy and happiness. Because Amy was going to be okay.

"I've got to get back," he said.

"Yes, go," she urged.

As he skirted past the tables, he thought about the miracle God had wrought on their behalf. The miracle of healing. But why couldn't the Lord heal Eva's broken heart? If only she could trust him. If only she could put aside her fears, they could be so happy together. But she'd told him no and he couldn't ignore the persistent ache in his chest.

He was leaving tomorrow. Leaving Eva behind. And as he stepped out into the cold night air, he felt empty and bereft.

Chapter Fifteen

The next morning, Eva shrugged into her short winter coat, tucked the heavy scarf around her neck and pulled on her warm leather gloves. Walking outside to the barn, she stood in front of Taffy's stall. The silver dappled gelding raised his head and gazed at her with brown, soulful eyes. As Eva opened the gate, Taffy snorted and backed up, as if to say it was too cold to go out for a ride today.

Eva persisted, slipping a halter over the horse's head and leading the animal out to the hitching post. Aunt Mamie was babysitting Cody for a few hours. Eva needed some time by herself. Needed to draw herself out of her doldrums. Tyler was leaving today. Word had spread around town that Amy Callister was doing great. There was nothing to hold Tyler here anymore, and Eva felt a bit lost and lonely because of it.

She slid a blanket onto Taffy's back, then hefted her saddle on. She pushed against the horse's chest, waiting a brief moment for the animal to exhale before cinching the saddle tight. She had everything she needed. She was so incredibly blessed. She didn't need marriage and kids in order to feel whole and happy. Yet she knew she'd never recover from loving Tyler.

Gathering the reins in one hand, she slid her booted foot into the stirrup and pulled herself into the saddle. Once she was seated, she turned the horse's head and clicked her heels. Taffy walked toward the east. They soon passed the row of barren oaks lining the dirt road. Frost glittered like white diamonds across the fields. The weatherman was forecasting rain in the next few days, so now was a good time to take a ride.

She galloped across an empty field, then rode beyond the farthest hills. Her body moved in easy rhythm with the gait of the horse. The ranch house and barn disappeared from view. It felt good to get away for a while. Good to be out in the open again. To be alone with her brooding thoughts.

Sometime later she pulled the horse to a steady walk. Her breath puffed on the air with each exhalation. Her heart felt heavy and broken, as though she would never be happy again.

Near the woods Eva tugged on the reins and pulled the horse to a stop. Resting one hand over the saddle horn, she inhaled the crisp morning air. Her nose and cheeks felt chilled, but not the rest of her. Only her aching heart. And she doubted there was anything she could do to warm that up. She needed time. To reconcile herself to being without Tyler. To not hearing his deep voice or seeing his handsome smile every day.

She looked over toward the field where they kept

their prized bull. His shiny black coat glimmered in the late morning sunlight. The enormous animal just stood and looked at her with stubborn patience. But Eva wasn't fooled. She knew firsthand that he could move like a flash of lightning if he wanted to. Her cousins had named him Fernando. As ornery as he was, Eva figured a different name would suit him better. He'd been known to charge without notice. After the trauma she'd suffered as a child, she had no use for bulls and had made a point of staying far, far away from them.

The stocky, cumbrous-looking animal stood near the white fence line, its curved horns long and sharp. A strange horse stood calmly grazing nearby. A dainty mare with two white stockings.

Hmm. That was odd. They never put horses in to graze with Fernando. He might get cantankerous and injure the horse. So, what were they doing in the same pasture together?

Eva tapped her heels against Taffy's sides. The animal stepped forward, taking Eva closer. She narrowed her eyes, gazing at the strange horse's rump, trying to make out the brand. A swinging *G*.

Eva gasped. No, it couldn't be. This horse belonged to Tyler. Was it possibly his stolen mare? But how had the animal got here? Where had it come from?

Eva glanced around, looking for some sign of other people. A truck or rider. Some explanation as to how Applejack had got into the same field with Fernando. The vacant fields and the hills beyond filled her view. She saw no one. Not a single soul to offer an explanation.

Eva rode nearer, noticing the gray hairs around the horse's muzzle and head. Maybe the thief had realized Applejack was an old horse, so he'd decided to turn the animal loose. And, of course, someone like her was bound to find the horse and get it back to its rightful owner.

A light of happiness clicked on inside Eva. Wouldn't Tyler be surprised? He and his mom would be so happy when they found out. They were not going to believe this turn of events. But how should she go about getting the horse out of the field with Fernando?

She gave the bull a dubious glare. He stared right back, not moving a single burly muscle. There was no way she was going into that pasture to get Applejack. Unfortunately, she'd left her cell phone at home, so she couldn't call anyone for help. She could ride back to the ranch and see if one of the hired hands would come back with her to retrieve the horse. But that could take a couple of hours and Eva didn't want to miss this chance. If the thief returned, the horse might disappear again. So, what were her options?

She stared at Applejack. Seeming completely unconcerned by Eva's predicament, the horse lowered her head and went back to grazing. Fernando did likewise, swishing his long tail as though irritated by her presence.

Eva took a deep, steadying breath and gripped the reins tight. She loved Tyler. She knew how much Applejack meant to him and his mother. She couldn't bear to turn her back on this opportunity. Not when it could bring the Graingers so much joy.

Thinking of Tyler, she gritted her teeth with determination. She was not leaving here without Apple-jack. It was that simple.

"Come on, boy." She tapped her heels against Taffy's sides and rode the horse over close against the gate.

She tightened her hands around the reins. Her fingers felt like sticks of ice in her leather gloves.

Bowing her head, Eva said a quick prayer. She asked for help. Asked for faith, safety and courage. And then she opened her eyes, determined to see this through. With God's help she could do anything. Even face her worst fear.

Lifting the latch, she opened the gate just enough for Taffy to ride through. A fissure of alarm rushed up her spine. If Fernando charged, she sure hoped Taffy was fleet of foot. As long as she stayed on her horse, she should be okay. But lots of bad things could happen. She'd learned that the hard way.

Moving slow and easy, Eva gave the bull wide berth, but she never took her eyes off the beast. The gentle clop of her horse's hooves striking the damp earth jangled her nerves. What if Applejack bolted? She'd have to chase after the horse and she didn't want to make any quick movements that might infuriate Fernando. What if her horse got spooked and bucked her off?

Thankfully, Applejack didn't run. Eva didn't even have to get off her horse as she reached for a lariat on her saddle and looped the lasso over the mare's head. Still riding Taffy, she quietly led Applejack back to the gate.

Fernando grunted and took a step. Eva flinched, her eyes flying wide. She fought off the urge to panic, to kick her horse into a run. To abandon Applejack and flee as fast as she could go.

She forced herself to remain calm. It took every ounce of willpower not to wave her arms or kick the horse into a frantic run. Taffy kept moving at a fast walk and Eva thought perhaps the gelding sensed her urgency.

They reached the gate and Eva led Applejack through. Only when she'd closed and secured the latch did she breathe a sigh of relief. She'd done it. She'd overcome one of her greatest fears. She'd defeated the foe and won the prize. She had Applejack.

Now she had another fear to face. Seeing Tyler again wouldn't be easy, but she had to do it. Had to ride over to his ranch one last time. It was late enough in the morning that he might have already left town. And maybe that would be for the best. She wouldn't have to see him again. Not ever. And that thought left her feeling lost and hollow inside.

"Okay, Mom. I think I'm ready to go." Tyler stepped into the living room and gave his mother a half smile.

"Are you all loaded?" Veola asked.

He nodded.

She was standing next to the sofa, and her chin quivered. Her lips scrunched and her eyes glistened with tears. "Oh, son. I wish you didn't have to go."

She threw her arms around him in a tight hug. He held her close, breathing in her warm familiar smell of cookies and cold cream.

"I'll be home for Christmas. You can count on that," he promised.

She drew back and wiped her eyes. "But it's not enough. I wish I could see you every day."

"I'm only a few hours away."

She frowned. "It's still too far."

He smiled and patted her soft cheek. "I know, Mom. I love you. And you can call me anytime, day or night."

She pursed her lips, obviously trying to be brave. "I know. I love you, too, son. I just wish you could—"

The doorbell rang, cutting her off.

Tyler turned, surprised that someone would come calling. Most of his patients knew he was leaving, but perhaps there was a straggler.

Stepping over to the door, he opened it wide, conscious of Mom standing just behind him.

"Eva!"

She stood there wearing her heavy coat and riding boots. A red knit cap was pulled low over her head, her cheeks bright from the cold. His heart gave a giant leap. Maybe she'd reconsidered his offer and realized they should be together. Maybe…

"What are you doing here?" His thoughts scattered like autumn leaves in the wind. He only knew he was thrilled to see her again. That he didn't want to let her go.

She gestured toward the front hitching post. He looked over her shoulder and his mouth dropped open. Applejack was tethered to the railing beside Eva's horse.

Mom gasped. "Why, that's our Applejack!"

"Yes!" Eva cried. "I just found her."

Grabbing their coats off the hooks by the door,

Tyler and Mom stepped out onto the porch. They hurried with Eva over to the horses, listening as she explained how she'd found the mare grazing in a remote field near the woods and her efforts to bring Applejack home.

"Oh, Eva! Thank you so much." Veola hugged her tight.

Tears streamed down the woman's face as she patted the horse, pressing her face against the animal's warm neck. Applejack nickered softly in response.

Tyler caressed the mare's head and soft muzzle. "I can't believe this. I can't believe you brought our horse home."

He looked at Eva, his heart overwhelmed with happiness and love. Out of his peripheral vision, he saw his mom back away.

"I'll leave you two alone to talk for a while. I'll be in the house if you need me." Veola turned and made a beeline for the front porch. She almost skipped with glee, and Tyler had no doubt she was ecstatic by this turn of events.

He faced Eva. She looked away. Looked at the horses, the barn, the house. Anywhere but at him.

"Eva, you really went into the pasture with Fernando?"

She nodded and a croaking laugh escaped her throat. "Yes, I did. And I've never been so scared in all my life."

Reaching out, he took her hand in his. "My brave Eva. I know what that must have cost you."

Her eyes filled with uncertainty and she stepped back. He dropped his hand away.

"I'm so glad you're here," he said. Anything to delay his trip. And he realized how badly he dreaded leaving.

She glanced over at his truck and the travel trailer hitched on behind. "It looks like I caught you on your way out of town."

"Yes, but I've changed my mind," he said, taking her hand again.

Finally, she met his gaze. "What do you mean?"

"I'm not going."

Another quizzical frown. "You're not going to Austin?"

"That's right. I'm staying right here with you."

She withdrew her hand and stepped back again. "No, Tyler. Please don't stay on my account. I can't marry you. I won't."

He stepped forward, pursuing her. Unwilling to let go. The moment he saw her, he knew it was futile to pretend. He loved her. He couldn't leave. Not now. She was everything to him. What good was living in a city all alone? With no one to love? It'd be the biggest mistake of his life. He knew that deep in the core of his soul.

"You brought me back to God," he said.

She blinked in surprise. "I think you found the Lord by yourself. I didn't do anything at all."

"That's not true. Your faith helped me see that anything is possible. That God loves us all, no matter what. Until I went to church with you last Sunday, I hadn't realized how much I'd missed the Lord in my life. How much I need Him. I have you to thank for bringing me back."

"I'm so glad to hear that."

And the Lord had blessed Amy, too. The little girl was completely on the mend. Smiling and gaining strength every hour. And Tyler realized anything was possible. Even healing his broken heart. He didn't feel angry anymore. He just felt anxious not to lose Eva.

"Tell me something. Do you love me?" he asked.

Eva went very still. She stared at him, her eyes bright. He wanted to take her into his arms, to warm her. Wanted to stay here in Little Horn and build a family with her.

"I…I can't, Tyler. I'm sorry. I can't give you what you want," she said.

His heart shattered. But he didn't believe her. Not after everything they'd shared. He loved her so much. Surely she felt the same way about him. If only she'd say the words. He could face anything in this life as long as he had Eva's love. Otherwise, no amount of pleading or groveling would do him a bit of good.

"I've got to go now," she said. "Aunt Mamie will be wondering what on earth happened to me. I've got to get back home to Cody."

She turned and reached for her horse. He stood there in a haze of hurt and disbelief, watching as she gathered up the reins and stepped up onto the gelding.

"Please don't go, Eva. I love you. Can't we work this out? If you love me, too, that's all I need."

She turned and faced him, but her gaze rested on the distant horizon. "Don't love me, Tyler. Please don't. Just go to Austin and forget about me."

Tapping her horse with her heels, she rode off. Tyler watched her go. He couldn't believe he was losing her. But he couldn't lose what he'd never had. Could he?

She didn't want him, and he ached with the thought. He'd found his faith again, but it had come at a high price. God had saved Amy's life. Surely the Lord could touch Eva's heart, too. But as Tyler watched her riding out of his life, he didn't see how.

Chapter Sixteen

Eva stepped into the dining room at Stillwater Ranch and set the plates and eating utensils on the long oak table. She folded the napkins and placed them to the left of each plate. Dinner was rarely a big affair these days, but Aunt Mamie still liked a nice setting. A comfy gathering where Eva and her aunt could catch up on the day. But it was lonely without Ben and Grady here, and she couldn't help missing her two cousins.

Eva's mind kept going over her conversation with Tyler. Their last goodbye had been anything but pleasant for her. In fact, she'd hated it. Hated the panic she'd seen in his eyes and the hurt she'd heard in his voice. And she regretted it, too. Regretted what had happened to her as a teenager and its impact on her life. But she wanted Tyler to be happy. To have the life he'd always dreamed of, researching childhood immunizations with his partners. But maybe she'd made a mistake. Maybe she should go with him to Austin. She loved it here in Little Horn, but Tyler's leaving seemed to have taken all the joy with him. Maybe she should change her mind. Maybe...

"Eva?"

She turned. Aunt Mamie stood beside the window, her head tilted to one side. Through the filmy curtains, Eva could see that it was raining. Large drops of water that lashed the house with the wind.

"Yes?"

"You didn't answer me, dear. You must be lost in your thoughts," the elderly woman said.

Eva reached for the salt and pepper shakers and set them on the table. "I'm sorry. What did you ask me?"

Aunt Mamie straightened a chair. "I asked what Tyler said when you delivered Applejack to him this morning."

Eva busied herself laying out the silverware. She appeared calm and rational, but deep in her heart she thought perhaps she'd made another blunder. Her head told her that walking away from Tyler was the right thing to do. To let him go on with his life and find a woman who could give him the family he wanted and deserved. But her heart said an entirely different thing. She couldn't help wondering if she'd made a huge mistake.

"He was happy to have his horse back, of course," she said.

"Is that all?" Mamie rested a hand on her arm.

"Aunt Mamie, I'd rather not talk about it." Eva met her aunt's gaze, longing to tell her everything. That Tyler had expressed his love. That she'd refused him and probably broken his heart. And she hated herself for it. Because her own heart was broken, too.

Mamie cupped both of Eva's forearms, holding her in place. "Maybe you need to rethink your vow to never marry. I've seen the way that man looks at you. And it'd sure be a cold day before I could walk away from so much happiness."

"I should say so." Martha Rose stood in the doorway, one hand on her ample hip. "I can't believe you went into that pasture with old Fernando. I sure never would have done it. You've got nerves of steel, gal. Surely you've got the courage to face marriage, don't you?"

Eva felt cornered by the two women. Forced to confront her own emotions. She wasn't happy about this predicament. She loved Tyler, but he deserved kids. He deserved a bouncing, happy family. What if they married and years down the road he changed his mind? His biological clock would start ticking and he'd realize he wanted children and grandkids and the whole nine yards. And then he'd start to begrudge what Eva couldn't give him. Possibly even come to hate her. She couldn't live with that. No, not at all.

Yet maybe it wouldn't be like that. Maybe he really would be happy adopting their family. There was only one way to find out. And Eva so dearly wanted to take that chance. But now it was too late. Tyler was gone. He'd moved on and so must she.

"I'd rather not talk about it," she said again.

She walked around the table, avoiding the two women. But she couldn't avoid her heart. It went with her, up in her throat. She wanted to cry. To scream. To take back every word she'd said to Tyler. To tell him that she loved him. That she wanted to be his forever. She'd thought that if she pushed Tyler away, she wouldn't get hurt again. But she'd been wrong. The pain in her heart was like the thrust of a sword. And now she wouldn't know the joy, either. And that was when she realized she had to take the good with the bad. She couldn't separate the two. She had to be more trusting. Filled with love and faith.

The doorbell rang, but she didn't go into the living room. Aunt Mamie or Martha Rose would answer the door. She returned to the kitchen, wondering how she could undo this mess. Wondering if she should drive to Austin tomorrow and beg Tyler to accept her apology. She'd rather stay here in Little Horn, but the thought of losing him made her stomach churn. Somehow, she had to get him back. She had to make this right. Because living without Tyler and his love was worse than being safe and lonely.

She turned and there he was. Standing beside the kitchen sink. The place where all of this had started the day he'd soothed her burned hand. That had been the moment she must have fallen in love with him. Except that she'd fought it for so long. Refused to see what was right in front of her eyes: a love worth fighting for.

"Hi there," he said with a half smile.

"Tyler." She whispered his name on a sigh of relief. He hadn't gone back to Austin after all. He was still here, right in her very own home. And suddenly, the world was filled with amazing possibilities.

"What…what are you doing here?" she asked.

He shrugged. "Making a house call."

"But…but the baby's fine. He's down for his nap, but should be waking up soon."

Tyler took a step closer. "I'm not here to see Cody. I've got another patient with a heart problem and I need to have a consultation with you."

Confusion filled her mind. He needed to have a consultation with her? What on earth was he talking about? "I don't understand."

He brushed a jagged thatch of hair back from his forehead, looking nervous and hopeful at the same time. "Is there somewhere that we can talk in private?"

Eva glanced at Martha Rose, who stood in front of the stove holding a spatula. A wide grin curved the woman's mouth with glee. Aunt Mamie hovered in the hallway, easily within earshot. No doubt the two women were eager to hear every word. Eva thought about where she could take Tyler so they could have a modicum of privacy. The front porch came to mind, but it was raining and too cold to sit on the swing.

"Come out to the barn with me. I need to check on the horses anyway." She led the way, determined to put this matter to rest right now. Determined to settle it in her own mind and heart once and for all.

He followed her to the front door. On the way, she grabbed her winter coat and pulled it on. He assisted her, lifting the garment over her shoulders so she could zip it up. Then he followed her outside, stretching his long legs out to keep up with her brisk stride as she scurried toward the barn. The billowing wind cut right through her and she bit back a gasp. The storm was coming in with gusto.

Tyler's presence gave her a mixture of giddy joy and ominous doom. She took those few seconds to formulate what she wanted to say. And suddenly she felt deliriously content. Because Tyler was here. Because she had a second chance to make this right. To fight for her future happiness.

They covered the distance to the barn in a matter of seconds. He lifted the latch to the double doors and they stepped inside the warm barn. He pulled the doors closed and the wind died off immediately. She flicked on the overhead lights. Her knees were wobbling, so she sat on a bale of straw and crossed her arms. Taking a deep breath, she spoke before he could.

"Tyler, this isn't easy for me. I know it can't be easy for you, either."

He stepped near, boxing her in against the tack room where they kept the saddles and bridles. She realized her mistake too late. But she didn't want to run away this time. She wanted to stay right here. With him.

"You have that wrong. This is the easiest thing I've ever done," he said.

She swallowed, trying to be brave. To have faith. To trust in God one more time. "I thought you would have gone back to Austin by now."

He shook his head. "I told you earlier. I'm not going anywhere."

"So, you've got a new patient with a heart problem?"

"Yes, it's me. I'm suffering from a broken heart,

and I don't believe I can ever recover without your love."

She felt overwhelmed. His words brought tears to her eyes. He'd said exactly what she needed to hear right now. What she'd wanted him to say.

"All this time you've been encouraging me to trust in the Lord. To have faith. And I think maybe you need to take some of your own advice," he said.

"You do?" Her voice sounded small and filled with awe. Which was appropriate, since that was how she was feeling right now.

"Yes, I do. I've spent the afternoon making phone calls. I've told my partners in Austin that I won't be joining them after all. They'll have to make do without me, because I'm staying right here in Little Horn. For good."

She released a croaking laugh. "But why would you do that? A life in the city is what you've always dreamed of. What you wanted."

"Not anymore. I want you. I could move back to Austin and do just fine. We'd both go on living our lives just fine. We might even be happy. But I've chosen to stay here. I can build my career in Little Horn. It's a choice, Eva. A choice I've made. It isn't right or wrong, but it's what I want to do with my life. And I feel so happy and peaceful now that I've made this decision."

She clutched her hands together in her lap, not sure if she was shaking from the cold or in reaction to his words. Maybe both. "Are you…are you sure that's what you want?"

He nodded, his eyes filled with tenderness and

love. "I'm absolutely, positively certain it's what I want to do. I even went into town this afternoon and rented some space where I can set up a nice medical practice. I've been practicing medicine out of my home long enough. The rooms in town will suffice until I can build my own office somewhere. I'm staying no matter what."

She stared. She couldn't move. Couldn't breathe. But he didn't push her for a response. He simply waited. Long, pounding seconds ticked by as she absorbed what he'd told her. And the ramifications of his choice. And then she realized he wasn't leaving. He wasn't going anywhere. He'd taken steps to make his life here in Little Horn permanent, to show his commitment to her. Something her ex-fiancé had never done.

"But what about your work in Austin? You have a grant from the FDA to do research. You have so many plans. A career."

"I have a career here. And it's been highly rewarding. I've spoken to my partners in Austin and I've also called our contact at the FDA. They've agreed that I can deepen our research by staying here and studying childhood immunizations and their impact on autism in rural communities. I can bless the lives of so many people right here in my hometown. I'm happy here, Eva. I couldn't ask for anything more... except for you."

Okay, here it was. She braced herself, determined to work this out. To have courage.

"But I can't have children, Tyler. I can't give you the family we both would love," she said.

He stepped nearer. "Yes, you can, sweetheart. We can have everything we both desire. All you have to do is say *yes*. I know you love little Cody like your own. Do you think I could feel any differently if we were to adopt a sweet baby like him? I could take him into my heart and home just like that." He snapped his fingers for emphasis.

He reached into his pocket and pulled out a small, black box. Eva stared. She would have gasped, but she couldn't move. Couldn't think a coherent thought right now. This wasn't what she'd expected. It had to be a dream. An illusion. Surely she'd wake up and find that it was all her wishful thinking run amok.

He reached out and took her hand in his. "I love little Amy Callister. And my other patients, too. Maybe it's my work as a pediatrician, but I love children. I always have. That stems from my little sister, when I lost her. Children are so precious. Even the Savior loved them dearly. We can adopt, Eva. In my line of work, I have some helpful contacts. People that can assist us in adopting as many children as we want. There are so many kids out in the world that need a loving home. But what I don't have is you."

"Oh, Tyler. I want to believe you. I truly do," she said. "But Craig said he could adopt and then he changed his mind at the last minute. How can I ever be certain that you won't do the same? I can't go through that pain again. I just can't."

"And you won't, sweetheart. Because I'm here and I'm staying. Even if I have to pay a house call out here every day to convince you that we should be together. You're not getting rid of me. Not ever."

Yes, she believed him now. Because she wanted to believe him. Because she wanted a future with him. She remembered all the times she'd seen Tyler with Cody. The gentle way he cared for Amy and his other patients. This was a man who loved children. All children. Just as the Lord loved them.

But there was no way that Tyler could prove to her that he wouldn't leave her, unless she first took a leap of faith. And then the day-to-day living, year after year, was how they both proved to one another that they were committed to each other. That they would always be there. That they would never leave. And she so badly wanted to take a chance on love again. She wanted to take a chance on Tyler.

"My love is different from Craig's," he said. "My love is built on faith and trust and respect. We've both been hurt before, but now we have each other."

"There's so much trouble in the town right now," she said.

"Yes, you're right. Cattle rustlings, thefts, Ben's in a coma, and Grady's in Afghanistan. I'm sure our lives will be filled with many trials and difficulties. But it's all going to be okay. As long as you and I are together, we can survive anything. God has given us a second chance. We need to have faith in Him and in each other. And so I'm asking you one more time. Eva, do you love me?"

He waited. The wind beat against the walls outside, blustery and whipping about so fiercely. But Eva barely noticed. She felt warm and protected here with him. Safe and loved.

"Yes," she finally said.

He cocked his head to one side. "What's that? Did you say *yes*?"

She gave a croaking laugh and hurled herself into his arms. "Yes, I love you. So very much."

He enfolded her in his arms, held her tight. She turned her face against the curve of his neck, breathing him in. Kissing him there.

"Oh, my dear Eva. Will you please marry me?" he asked.

"Yes," she whispered desperately. "Yes!" she said again, much louder this time, throwing her inhibitions to the wind. It was time.

He laughed, and then he kissed her lips.

"Oh, Eva. My sweet Eva." He laughed, the sound deep and filled with absolute bliss.

"There's just one problem," she finally said.

He cupped her face with his hands and looked deep into her eyes. "And what's that, sweetheart?"

"I can't cook. Not at all. You know that, right?"

He laughed. "Yes, I know. It's a good thing I can. I think we'll be fine."

He finally released her and went down on both knees. Opening the box, he showed her a sparkling diamond ring.

"I want to do this right. To bow down and humble myself before you. To make sure you know how serious I am and how much I want you. Eva, will you marry me?" He lifted the ring high.

She nodded, her eyes filled with tears of joy. "Yes, Tyler. Oh, yes. I will."

He slid the ring onto her finger. And then she was

in his arms again, kneeling with him in the clean straw. Breathless with joy.

He kissed her forehead, her cheeks, her lips. And then he just held her and rocked her within his arms. Never had she felt so cherished. Such happiness. Such absolute love.

The wind and a thud against the barn brought her back to the present. A storm was coming in, but inside her heart, she felt absolute peace.

"I guess we should go back inside the house. I'm sure your aunt will be wondering what's going on. And Martha Rose, too," he said.

"Yes, but not just yet," she said. "I want a few more minutes alone with you. To cherish this time for as long as I live."

Pulling her cheek close against his heart, he clasped her tight within his arms. And she realized this moment didn't have to end. She felt enveloped in harmony and trust. Because she belonged right here. She was his now. For always and forever.

* * * * *

If you liked this
LONE STAR COWBOY LEAGUE *novel,*
watch for the next book,
A RANGER FOR THE HOLIDAYS
by Allie Pleiter, available December 2015.

And don't miss a single story in the
LONE STAR COWBOY LEAGUE *miniseries:*

Dear Reader,

When my husband and I were first married, we planned to have five children. We wanted enough members in our family that we could make an entire basketball team. We were young and in love and so happy. But then I lost three babies in a row. As men often are, my husband was more pragmatic about it. But I was brokenhearted. It was several years before we were able to have a precious little boy of our own. And after that, nothing. We didn't lose any more babies, but we didn't get pregnant again, either. So, we adopted a beautiful six-day-old baby girl. My two children are both grown and married now, but I thank God for them every day. They are two of my greatest friends.

In *A Doctor for the Nanny*, the heroine is broken-hearted because she believes she can't have what she wants the most: a family of her own. Following a childhood accident that took her ability to give birth, and then being abandoned at the altar by her fiancé because he doesn't want to adopt in order to have kids, she doesn't think any man will ever want her now. But she learns some valuable lessons about faith and trust. She learns that we all are children of God. That He loves each and every one of us. And that adoption is a gift of the heart. A blessing that fills empty arms and repairs shattered dreams. I thank the Lord that one special woman was selfless enough to give her baby to me to raise and make my own.

I hope you enjoyed reading *A Doctor for the Nanny*, and I invite you to visit my website at www.LeighBale.com to learn more about my books.

May you find peace in the Lord's words!

Leigh Bale

REQUEST YOUR FREE BOOKS!

2 FREE INSPIRATIONAL NOVELS
PLUS 2
FREE
MYSTERY GIFTS

Love Inspired®